Valley of Flowers

a novella

CHRIS COLLINS

for India

(no A.I. was used in its creation)

ISBN 978-0982394960

For more on this book and others go to @CollChris on X or use hashtags #VOF or #ValleyofFlowers.

CONTENTS

1 | *Garden on Top of the World*

The Valley of Flowers ahead looked awash in sunrays and colourful wildflowers. All seemed so expertly arranged and crowding the valley in thousands and millions there would be no counting their number. Dew-gilded gleaming flowers appeared in maximum bloom. The glare captivated him and his senses took flight. Nicolas Kumar had arrived.

His trek journey had brought him to this mountain place on a crisp cool morning that was his birthday. The scene presented lent a warm ambiance to his interiors. However, he might have preferred his father had gifted him a brand new BMW.

The 17-year-old Indian youth, tall, pinch-fit from regular workouts, held up to take a breather as a couch potato. He felt the blunt chill of low temperatures. In front of his face, puff clouds formed and dissipated from his outgoing breath. His hope now was for getting a good solid round up here, on first seeing this famed valley's primal beauty.

Once more the school-going teenager breathed in deep that stretched his lungs to the utmost. In among the fresh, sweet open air was a fragrant scent he took deep in his lungs. He exhaled while setting down his rucksack in a freestanding display. His breathing became more normal then and he felt reassured. Now he felt being up in the Indian Himalayas was a timely step for him and one in the right direction.

Nicolas took off his red fleece jacket, wrapped around his waist, and he laid it onto his standing pack. In a no-hurried manner, he removed his cap and ran his fingers through his thick brown hair. His skin and his wavy hair were a similar colour brown, with his skin darkened from the many hours out in the sun on the practise range, and while out on the course during play.

His dark eyebrows shielded his curious and eager slate-grey eyes that were good and quick, sharper for sighting his long wood and iron shots out of mid-air, and from spotting the errant ones lying in the long grass.

Nicolas returned his cap atop his head and crooked it with finger and thumb. He added more bend to the bill's centre. He looked to the many-flowered valley. He received bales full of colourful garlands, as each timeless frame-to-frame picture in his mind's eye without exception solicited then obtained from him a brief promise to stay, and never again return to the jungle of concrete and commotion, roads or dividing walls, nor ever go back to the unholy rolling on juggernaut of live wire.

Nicolas stared at the scene of immortal bliss and searched its tranquil wonders. Glee came through to make him smile.

His readiness for the approaching contest suffered some from this giddiness, as he stood self-consciously on the tee box square, gratification of the senses his highest goal.

'Teledensity has certainly not reached here,' whispered the mostly city-centric youth.

Favouring pink Himalayan balsams, in a valley far from the maddening urban crowds, the plush sea of alpine flowers appeared in palpable excitement over the possibilities of this one fine day in paradise.

Dotted here and there purple and blue, and raised from the Earth, here a blue poppy, there a cobra lily and edelweiss, the flowers seemed on proud glorious display in an absolute must-have bouquet, and all looked nourished by a fast-running stream, rushing through a slight middling valley.

The spill off came from an in-the-distance small lake. Its check-dams appeared filled to the brim and stemming from a spectacular waterfall, flowing like champagne and then Oh, a rainbow! The rainbow added shape to this cut cake, ordered for the occasion of charmed magic, and all got his mind into feeling divine timelessness and just right disarray.

Nicolas gazed at this sparkle. He took in the invigorating crisp clean air and view of a lifetime. He wondered who coloured these many flowers. Consequently, he fought for ownership of this prime piece of land. The battle within him, however, did not last long. Inside, his immediate plan to claim this superb, untamed property was simply to roll out the world's best drive.

Nicolas closed his eyes in a pretend moment. He rested a hand against his encasing chest. Again he breathed in deep. Nicolas resumed telecasting from this high place and great advertising space. He remembered with pleasure then one remarkable achievement, and what he recalled was his own qualifying for the Open Championship, only a fortnight back. This story of success repeated in his mind. He felt pleased with himself also for making it all the way up here without hiring a *piththoo*, or porter with a basket, to carry his pack or even himself.

Again, Nicolas peered out at the valley and his eyes moistened. His eyes went wide in the shadows under his red cap or company-branded hat canopy. The valley looked quite peaceful, strikingly ablaze with sizzling pinks, stimulating blues, elegant electric greens, along with all-accompanying sunbeam yellows, with a smart sporty feel, and gone forever here, it seemed, were the big city's basic beiges where proud materialists reside.

'Whoever drafted this course must have seen the brighter side,' Nicolas said aloud to no one. And look, what colours! Nothing I have ever known can compare with this. He then added a bit from the weatherman in him. And what a day this is too! The sky is nearly without blemish. You do not get many days like this, I should think.

Nicolas sensed something was missing. The presence of his father, his classmates and teachers, the city he always said he owed his success, were now all on his mind. But then he was taken in wholly again by this colourful flowered valley, while feeling strangely apart from it too.

Nicolas stood on the 1st tee as any nervy freshman on the first day of school. He felt it would take some time to come to terms with this illustrious new environment. He thought anyone would need a little orientation session here, akin to receiving a handheld walkthrough of the area.

The thought of receiving help reassured him. It ignited in him the strong wish to make it back home, preferably in one piece, and not far off into the future, and that his father would no longer be angry at him. This jogged his memory more into recalling his spoilt days of childhood.

Nicolas Kumar, a destiny's child, born with a silver spoon in his mouth, recalled the seventh-heaven habit of being picked up after by doting as well as adoring servants, as with last summer, when he received a Bullet motorbike to ride around on, but only under a servant's supervision and just in the family yard. Now he thought all summers were blemish-free cards, filled with oceans of love and happiness.

He stood then in chilly wonder. He enjoyed this reliving of the happy days. Nicolas thought of his father at the time of qualifying for the Open Championship.

2 | *The Game*

"Father, I have qualified for the British Open!"

Before Nicolas came bursting into the clubhouse with his glad announcement, his father had been debating with friends on who was the best ever to play the game. Names of players both past and playing today were mentioned. His father had even offered his own gentle son.

And while the discussion participants were accustomed, chained-to scholars of the game that provokes and maddens, immersed in solemn contemplation at one moment, then eagerly arguing a point in another, the question was going mostly unanswered.

When one brought up the name of a player playing in the present, this was opposed with the argument that this player has enjoyed playing with better equipment than those who had come before. When a player from the distant or not too distant past was suggested, it was argued that this player had enjoyed playing when there was far less competition, as the game's popularity was not nearly so great.

As the debate was heading this way, to a most uncertain conclusion, Nicolas Kumar, his admirers pleased with fame and victory and the crowd's loud voice emerging behind him, interrupted his father again with his proud declaration. This stunned the crowd into a formal awkward hush. Only when he insisted on speaking out of place, by repeating his statement yet one more time, did Nicolas receive a response from his much-loved father.

His father smiled at first. He put on an even bigger 32-teeth display. He spoke his words clearly, firmly, to his son and for all to hear.

"Nicolas, it seems your ego is getting the best of you. Go now, and give it to death."

Following this, the next several days at home were spent preparing for this departure. Nicolas Kumar, confused and heartbroken, begged his father's forgiveness and for some explanation. But none were given. In their place he was told where to begin his journey and which way to go. He was told what conditions he could expect once there and to gather all the supplies he felt he could reasonably carry on such a high mountain trip. He was also told to do it at once.

Mournfully, he sat alone in what was now the punishment corner of his room. Sadly, he turned his head towards the wall as to join with an imaginary other. He remained this way in a type of commiserating huddle. He had the feeling of being fastened to this unhappy other character. Nicolas struggled to catch some understanding of his hurts, feelings of brokenness and resentments, along with his marring bitterness.

Some time passed before he rose by will. Nicolas went over to his study table to make out a list of things he wanted to have with him in the mountains. When this list became too long, he tore it up and threw it out. Again he conjured up a catalog of essentials and this list too was made overlong.

At about this time, Nicolas pleaded out loud for the kitchen to come serve him. He called for a plate of croissants, along with a masala omelet and juice to be brought to him. Soon after, he was enjoying another worthy entrée. He gobbled up precious pancakes, soaked in delectable syrup, along with hot-melted butter that was presented to him inside his room.

That done, he felt more or less ready to get down to the business of preparing. He directed his mind next to a single task without mood swing and soon found a solution there.

He would begin with a number.

He began with the weight he knew he could carry: twenty kilograms. He added two kilos to this. As his clubs would be the heaviest items in his pack, Nicolas went about seeing to them to start.

Along with his three wedges, two woods and a putter, he considered minimising his tote by taking with him only the odd-numbered irons, though not a 1-iron as he did not carry one. He reasoned that if a shot required an 8-iron, he could either jump on a nine or ease off a seven. As for retaining both woods, Nicolas hoped to take advantage of the added distance the thin mountain air offered as there would be no telling how long some holes might be up in the Himalayas.

Driver included, he felt quite capable hitting his woods off the fairway. He felt confident too, given reasonable lies, he could achieve good height on most shots hit with them.

Once more he reviewed his club selection. He lingered on the idea of flat refusing one of his three recovery-agent wedges. Faced with the decision of leaving behind his lob wedge, his sand wedge or his pitching wedge, Nicolas was not as certain as he had been with his standard irons. The difference in shot length between his lob wedge and sand wedge was approximately twenty meters. The difference between his sand wedge and pitching wedge was another thirty meters, and not the concern. What Nicolas wanted from them most were their cutting blades, unique to each, with varied uses, and specially customised for him.

Finally he decided to retain all three. Nicolas determined he would not want to be faced with a greenside recovery shot when one of the left-behind wedges was clearly required.

Believing his selection had been sensibly made, he pulled from his bag the chosen clubs of his regular set. He took them to the rice vendor for weighing at the outdoor market. When Nicolas asked to weigh the clubs, the rice seller gave him a questioning look.

'What is the use of these sticks?' asked the mustachioed vendor, placing the clubs onto the weighing scale.

One answer came from the vegetable stall next door that was the market hub. 'Police truncheons,' said the vegetable seller, handing a bag of onions to a customer.

'Made special for the Centre,' affirmed the happy customer accepting the goods.

Nicolas explained the use of the weighed clubs. And while still distraught over his current bleak plight, he marvelled too then that even in this mega city, in this modern day and age, there were still those who did not know the enslaving game known as golf, or even himself now, Nicolas Kumar, idol to tens of thousands, made most famous recently by his name and image being broadcast round the world.

The scale read just over four kilograms, and though he had the expectation of a higher number he was not pleased with the amount. Savings in weight, he reasoned, would have to come elsewhere.

Eventually he would carry a modified-down pack (670g) that would include other ultra-lightweight camping gear, such as a goose-down sleeping bag (960g), with a liner and pad (400g), one silicone-flyweight tent, yellow, with soft pegs and weighing 1.2 kilograms, along with a water bottle, full, weighing just under two kilograms, a less-than-a-litre cooking pot (120g), a bowl, a pint-sized cup with a spoon, 5 x 10 binoculars, a medical kit, rope and small knife, a 288 rupee grey umbrella, plus a torchlight and lighter, a fold-up shovel, sunglasses and sun cream, a sun cap to protect him from the burning high-altitude sun, a toothbrush and tooth powder, some soap and a quick-dry towel.

Nicolas would have with him too a dozen-and-a-half golf balls (45g each) arranged in the box as a truncated triangle, 3 4 5 6. He would bring with him too cold weather clothing, like a windcheater and gloves, an extra pair of briefs, dry-fast synthetic socks, black polypropylene tights, shell pants or overtrousers, one long-sleeved T-shirt, beneath a dark-blue pullover, coupled with his red jacket and clutch pack.

And because he liked them, since they were already well-broken in, the hiking boots he planned to wear would be the waterproof Italian-made pair his father had brought back for him from Nepal.

The youth always wore a watch on his left wrist when he played, and for this trip too he would have with him round his neck a small compass in the form of a red whistle.

As for food he would buy most of it in the hilltop village at the start of his trek. All together he judged the food would weigh four kilograms. It would consist of muesli, flat round breads, two-minute noodles, freeze-dried veggies, pasta, beans and rice. Powdered milk would also be incorporated. Nicolas Kumar would have with him his all-important tea, a mixed bag of nuts, a complement of chocolate bars, all of which would be available at the hill station's *kirana* store.

Preparations too, he knew, included leaving his much-loved father.

For this career timeout, he carried on thinking up the worst possible scenarios and tried planning for them. He prepared for any and all unknowns. And there was little time. Soon approaching was his overnight train journey, then bus ride further up the mountain, leading the next day to a showtime Wednesday morning that was, to him anyway, Moving Day.

He returned in his mind to this garden paradise. He came back to this 1st tee where community members from the lower village had, decades ago, brought up two bronzed pots to work as tee markers. On the slopes of the valley, he noticed a few pint-sized trees, their limbs with their leaves blowing in the occasional whipped-up cool breeze. Nicolas felt this high garden was a faultless example of what could be achieved on Earth: an oasis of perfect peace, plain and simple.

He took more note of the astonishing flower concentration. Nicolas gazed at all that was arrayed under a brilliant sun. He believed all had been set there just for him.

3 | *His Multi-Coloured Umbrella*

Just then Arjuna emerged carrying a large conch onto the tee-block platform. He made his self present amidst this incredible earthly activity on tremendous scale. Walking and breathing with effort, underneath the illuminative shade of his multi-coloured umbrella, he gratefully unsaddled and set down his pack, his self sitting and resting on it. He sat ruling the roost from there in the centre of this fantasma.

Arjuna had on a boyish grin on a deeply tanned face. His experienced smiling eyes, great gifts from having seen so much of the world with a balanced attitude, showed bright while sparkling intense depths. The old man's hair looked like puffs of white clouds, not too unlike Lord Indra's who playfully stole heavenly cows in the old Vedas tale. His hair behind his ears had the colour of clouds also, but was a touch rain-bearing.

Arjuna was kitted out in synthetic black pants that were modern and popular for trekking. To Nicolas, the old man appeared more familiar with the age of silk ties, plus fours, and argyle socks. Arjuna wore a blue down jacket, to keep himself warm in the cool mountain air, and draped around his neck was a pale-white shawl. The hand-spun pashmina shawl rose and fell some with his down jacket reacting to his lungs taking in repeated deep breaths.

The old man nodded in a kindly way. He raised a hand to signal a short break or perhaps start up like the band. This somewhat smiling elder held out for more air then while resting.

For having entered the valley of immortal bliss, Arjuna straightaway had the cheerful suspicion from the old myth of being carried off by nymphs and fairies. He delighted more in large dollops of mysticism.

Arjuna wondered what additional mysteries were contained in the age-old stories from here, recorded in the holy tracks he so cherished.

With a touch of bewilderment, Arjuna half-expected trained musicians with flutes, maestros from the Gwalior *gharana*, accompanied by hip-shake dancers, bedecked in red-and-white saris, with their tinning bangles, jingle-bell anklets, and cheering enthusiastically, to come swooping down on the wind, roll off onto this flowerful carpet, or glitzy affair, to stand positively before him while performing in 3/4 time.

'Look!' cried Nicolas, standing at the front of the tee box. 'Isn't it beautiful?' And with a sweep of his arm he added a slow stroke over this celebrated land.

Just off the tee was a blue-flower cluster. From this patch of blue poppies, growing out inexplicably from a crackless stone, the old man's mind rose more above the material mundane. Arjuna's meditation was then on one blue leaf. He looked then to a grown-up patch of grass. The grass stood near the stone from which these flowers grew.

Among the luminaries present, a butterfly fluttered about. The butterfly gave this nature lover the chance to observe near at hand the fine art of flying.

Arjuna watched this flier flit from flower to flower and for a moment he marvelled, wondering gladly, though not for the first time, how this one fine thing was indeed possible. He felt not love for this poetic gathering of butterfly, rock, flower, along with his humble self, but a joyful anxiety, characterised as the will to do something in this world and make some difference.

Arjuna next considered worthwhile a strategy to serve, or at least put a smile on the faces of these citizen creatures for here.

The old man flouted more this norm or strong feeling to give back. He held out an upturned hand. He wished to give a good landing place to this butterfly and O so valiant flier. His sight ascended five thousand kilometers then, as Arjuna looked to the grand eternal expanse or near-bottomless blue business that was this morning's sky.

The old man peered lower, towards the current pantheon of telling points. Arjuna looked to the mountain range's seven snow-clad peaks. He gazed at the constructed castle spree up in the crisp cool air. These mountains seemed prone also to long-term fits of melancholy.

His focus came back, though not resting on one flower cluster, or swath of blue poppies, brilliantly illumined and standing sprightly out of a solid stone. Nor was his focus on this colourful communion, where the gods had tossed down flowers as darts for over millennia, but on the minute.

Just then the ground before him abruptly broke open.

Through the popped-up tuft of grass a single stem rose. At first this one flower came up unsteadily. It went on to put out boldly though the hard knot of a new bud.

Arjuna watched this miracle of life grow. The old man saw it rise, struggle to mature, amidst the elements and the ever-present life changes. He leaned in to get a closer look. He wanted to study better a water bubble that had miraculously formed on one fragile leaf.

To Arjuna, the reverse image that showed on the bubble's face reflected well a delicate avant-garde or work that is experimental.

The old man felt the tinge of apprehension. He fretted some over the fate of this one flower with the O so subtle gleam. He was concerned its shine could be broken by so much as a tiny scratch from a butterfly's foot.

The flower reached some peak. The old man felt blessed for having seen this beauty grow up, evolve amidst all here, then age. Arjuna watched this one flower begin to wilt. He observed it bending low, onto the ground now, to die.

'Yes,' he said, to answer the youth's original question. 'What we resist persists in this miracle and daily informs us that much in this world is O so agreeably lovely.'

The comment supported and got keys to this earthly palace, which readily serves all, together with the coarse, the poor and downtrodden, the powerless and the voiceless.

'Well,' said the youth, fashioning to gain control of these pretty premises and he was fast on the look out now for this opportunity while the art market was still booming. 'If life is going to bring me this opportunity, and I do get my fair chance, I should do fairly well here.'

With this, Arjuna reached in his pack to rustle up an item to give this eager fellow. On finding it, he held the thing out for him to come take. 'Here,' Arjuna said. 'Inside there is a map provided with the descriptions of the holes you will encounter along the way. The map shows their lengths and their pathways to them. Do you have a compass with you?' he asked.

The youth felt through his shirt for the compass-as-whistle hanging round his neck. 'Yes,' he said cheerfully, stepping over to the old man.

'Good,' said Arjuna. 'Now I have written a few words for your record of play here. These hymns to the gods are meant to be heard. So, when you read them to yourself they will be heard! If you find they are useful to you, sing their praises by please using them.'

When Nicolas thought the old man was done speaking, he put his hands together at his chest meaning I recognise the god within you. He bowed then slightly, to this elder and teacher. He accepted the handmade coursebook with both hands. Nicolas did this as if receiving possession papers to a grand palace, or accepting the keys to creation, happy to get custody but sad too as he sensed that all this gift-giving might soon be over.

As the old man moved to sit more comfortably, the youth opened up his new course journal there and then. He began reading to himself Arjuna’s written mantra for this 1st hole, up on the Indian Himalayan course known as Truind.

There are various ways of warfare, not merely with simple metal weapons, having a reflective, meditative mind among them. Become expert in these many other ways. Begin your duty then, providing an unmatched contribution.

Nicolas concentrated on the note. He looked at its strange script for some significance. He mulled over one fragment of this teacher's words to arrive at some gist. Happy in the garden already, on a day made for doing endless somersaults, Nicolas felt the note in the handmade textbook was a series of meaningless lyrics to a song, so he lifted an eyebrow then shrugged.

'All right then,' he said not comprehending, though feeling quite the star or darling to the masses, and again he looked back down at this teacher’s curious say of words.

Once more his mind ventured out. But then he gladdened at this note that he felt had come from a loving lord. He told himself next to get serious and also to concentrate. Still, he seemed only ready to accept a funny one-liner. Nicolas felt performing on this mountain stage was all about having fun. The youth believed a series of triumphs were sure to be his. He made up more evidence that supported this view.

But just as Nicolas looked up from his course journal as a giggle-puss, there roused in him an element of curiosity.

This doubt puffed, swelled up to become a great cloud of suspicion, hanging as if over his head. Nicolas had no idea what the subject matter was. This left his thinking like the breeze, in something of a drift.

A cool wave of air swept through to chill and even buckle up his skin The mystery note had not gone away. It held up motionless, ordinary, markedly self-denying as any vacant cartoon bubble, when just then a solitary message appeared in it as a *Pop!* in any Eureka moment.

This bolt-from-the-blue communication struck and pierced his exalting heart. It had him reeling under this red-flagged occasion. It spawned in him a simple though most urgent question.

Where is the fairway?

4 | *The Defender*

One answer came as a hard thud. This was followed fast by his quick-beating heart. Right before his eyes there seemed to be a severe paint-peeling going on. Nicolas staggered in his thoughts. He felt barely able to stand also, physically. If he toppled, Nicolas imagined he may appear as yet another hooch tragedy, emanating from one of the alcohol-selling Indian states. This marked well his extreme disappointment.

Nicolas looked eyes-glazed over the many-flowered valley. He peered at what had once been his exact image of perfect peace and absolute goodness. He scanned the multitude of wildflowers that sparked his fears. Nicolas looked dartingly there and there as any fear-based conditioned soul. Once a tall, 185 cm figure and proud, he felt greatly diminished.

He stood there in silence. He looked for any open space for his escape. He saw in the violent realities that there was no known room without occupying flowers. His hopes sank to their lowest lows. His eagerness now was plainly missing as with state funds being siphoned.

Nicolas inhaled deeply. He found all this hard to digest. What is this all about anyway? he thought. More words out of frustration may have come from him had there been no real self control. At this time he thought to cast himself in the role as a defender. He felt the flowers with their bright worried faces were like candles lighted in protest. He heard them raise hue and cry over the desecration issue.

Nicolas thought the time spent coming up this high heap had been thoroughly wasted. He looked down and drained. He was convinced that he would be heading back down the mountain soon. Nicolas once had dreams of idle perfection as on Mount Meru: object of solemn contemplation, centre of all that is physical, metaphysical, spiritual, on top the City of Brahma indescribable. He turned then to express his deep concern to Arjuna.

Having seen the change coming, the old man had readily risen. He looked prepared, standing, waiting calmly beside his small pack. The old man stood unmoving, not shuffling nor shifting about. He appeared ready and willing only, as with any good mentor, to accept whatever might come from the aggrieving youth. And Nicolas did speak.

'Sir, you confuse me,' he said in an upset voice. 'Am I to hit into these many flowers?'

'Destruction before creation,' said the old man tenderly, as in a condolence message. This communication had been delivered soft. It arrived, however, at the youth's doorstep as something of a norm-buster.

Nicolas felt he was at some life crossroads. He braced to cope. He stared at the vast array of flowers without having much hope for them. In the greying distance, where once he believed a population of lions still roamed, Nicolas Kumar replayed the message from this good teacher. Again it went off as a planted bomb. A moment of some silence passed between them. Both understood without thinking of it that silence in their culture was not at all offending. Still the quiet felt like an affronting whipped-up wind.

More seconds passed where each felt the other should say something. Arjuna caved in first. Initially, the old man broke the silence with a throat-clearing cough. He added a retiring line that denoted grave kindness. 'It is always this way,' he said, 'and in this way beauty calls.'

Nicolas was in turmoil, his eyes fixed and housed terror. He stood there in bits and pieces. It seemed like bricks and rubble had been strewn all round. He wanted a miracle and not a lot of explanations.

For his part, Arjuna resisted the base urge to try and solve the problem. He sought only to add to this type of correct code of conduct. Arjuna used his influencing strong voice that made starting play here seem almost mandatory.

'Finally,' said Arjuna, 'this is Shiva and this is love.'

At first, Nicolas tried to understand this fine nuance. Then he had on a look suggesting that even trying to understand this high philosophy would only boomerang back onto him. As playing here would be quite unjust, it occurred to him motivating others, to perhaps join some movement, would be his highest priority. It dawned on this peace promoter too that a candlelight vigil, set for the evening say, might help highlight the grave hazards in coming up here for this. Only at the last minute did Nicolas move away from saying aloud his wild slew of schemes.

He had no desire now to step on this many-flowered valley, or subtlest example of the Divine Mother's good grace. He looked to Arjuna for some change of heart. He saw only that the old man was ready to speak more.

'Now it's best for you not to know too much truth,' Arjuna said with some consternation, 'or concern yourself with too much understanding. If you were to know All, you would not for a moment think to harm another. This I'm quite sure. If you were to know All, a look of horror, Absolute Truth's first salvo, would bolt across your face in a lightning's flash. Maybe you would fall to your knees just then and bleat like sheep. Along my many life-wanderings I have seen this look numberless times. For you now, and it will not always be this way, moving toward wisdom is to do so by performing deed, for yourself and for All That Is, and only by performing deed do you make truth be your vow. These are the words I care to express to you. So enjoy heatedly then, by getting out there and performing, as there can be no substitute, all the while remembering that from the four main points of the compass, as well as from above and below, life will come at you. So be ready.'

Arjuna allowed a few seconds to pass before speaking more. He gifted himself this break to take in a quantity of air. He replenished sufficiently his expended breath. Then he went back into the hunt.

'Now I ask you, Nicolas, what are you hesitating about? Go on and take on this battle. Get into the game now and carry out your born-into promise.'

The youth looked out at the wildflowers or sea of distressed humanity. This had him thinking he was not yet ready for this horrific hand and foot action.

I cannot think of such an act, he told himself. To say that I would even consider playing here is really quite scandalous. Nicolas felt certain that hitting into these bands of colourful sharp dressers was not at all one of his options.

He wished to escape from this high place. Nicolas had the urge to retire to a life of quiet contemplation. The youth stepped up ways to do away with his current situation. In a repeated message, he told himself, and angrily this time: Just end this thing and head back! Then he wondered how it may be to send his drive into this colourful perfumed lot.

No, he thought. Hitting into this pretty valley, which seems to accept all that comes its way, is something I cannot see myself doing. And he discarded the notion wholesale.

There is only one choice to make, Nicolas told himself, steady and sure. The choice is either to enter and begin play here or do not at all.

One plan stood out prominently in his mind. It was to give an apology to this good teacher, leave here quietly and be back home at the earliest. This was acted out first inside his head. Then, without thinking much more of it, he openly said so. He looked to Arjuna and told him plainly.

'I'm sorry if you have been inconvenienced. But I object to this.' And for a split moment all action escaped him.

Nicolas looked out at the many-flowered valley. The sight of ripe immortal peace in his path overwhelmed him with grief. He experienced a crisis in his own citizenship here. Nicolas Kumar, son of a thoughtful scholar though chemist by profession, possessing a blameless character, lifted his eyes just then to the silvered heights for guidance. All came to a standstill for him then as no help seemed forthcoming.

The youth stood feeling coltish. He wondered what more he can do. Inside, his heart ached. No hope pressed. One thing he knew he could do was put up a brave front in the face of this big playing meltdown.

How can fate be so unkind? he thought.

Again, Nicolas looked mournfully at the Valley of Flowers fairway. He sank down then, as if time and space had both collapsed. His back he held erect. The heel of his right foot pressed firm at the base of his spine and he said, 'I will not.'

5 | *An Indefinite Strike*

Nicolas sat planted as a seed or sampling might. In perfect silence he stayed still there, not moving and also not doing. By changing the form of a crucial verb, Nicolas, stricken, knew he had undertaken his firmest reservations here. He felt at the core of some supreme righteousness. He made believe he was calm and not that wounded. Nicolas planned to stay right where he was, sitting there doing not much. He looked ready for some good long fight ahead.

In demonstrating this *asan* from classical yoga, a practise to link up Self with God, he attempted next to have not one thought-desire.

Nicolas closed his eyes. He entered this region of pitch-black darkness. He set his mind for some compressed repair. To any who happened by, he was glad he might appear as one who is holy, an astute guru in his own right, unraveling the immense mysteries of the vast universe. He entertained next the idea of staying this way for all time. Nicolas felt he could stage this strike, or *dharna*, until hell froze him over. This could come in a few months' time, he quickly figured out, by the onset of an early winter.

A fresh moment passed where otherwise he may have been up and doing. Lid-blinded, he stared into dark chaos.

Nicolas felt the urge to act. He moved his forearms down onto his knees. His forefingers and thumbs touched to form a pair of neat circles. In this way he struck a near-perfect pose of achieved bliss, or perceived blessed joyousness. He got more settled. Nicolas hoped to show his nobleness more.

He sensed the flowers come in close. He opened his eyes. To him, the flowers looked as if they wished to thank him and to somehow aid him. They appeared to move in even closer. He next imagined that they were grateful for what he was doing for them now individually, as well as for the community as a whole. He sat feeling loved, surrounded by these colourful flower visitors.

The pulsating sea of wildflowers came in crushingly close then to try and compress him. He imagined them showing a friendlier *What's up!* attitude towards him. He sensed the flowers turn angrily west at him. The flowers appeared as a large crowd waiting on any railway platform. Nicolas made believe too that they were gathering expectantly for their final shuffle, sudden rush, push and hard shove, towards the one exhibiting the awe-inspiring bright light.

The youth created next a sense that railway police officers were present. He had the coppers take up positions over all in the valley. He had them holding up their *lathis*, or baton weapons, to be used on the flowers if needed.

He gave his attention next to these high mountain pillars. They stood as giant law-keepers over all in the valley. The Indian Himalayas outlined strikingly this area's extreme terrain that bordered on rich decadence. He was unhappy with the breeze coming in just then which no player worth his salt could ever really trust.

An electrifying charge permeated the chilly atmosphere. Nicolas again took refuge in his mind. He militated more against playing here. He considered a fast-unto-death. He cited under his breath, Nobody can dictate terms to me, Nicolas Kumar, recent qualifier of the Open Championship, not even this good teacher, learned as he appears to be.

Nicolas pondered this until realisation surely thumped him that he was indeed being asked to play into these flowers. He said aloud and defiantly, 'No, I cannot possibly. I cannot soil my hands by striking out at those near and dear to me.'

'And by pause do you defend your position any better in this world?' asked Arjuna. 'By not striking out, and entering this fray,' he added, 'do you—'

'Yes, but this is not a fairway!' erupted Nicolas, sensing no scope for mercy here. Then he said to himself, What could Father and this good fellow have been thinking! May God bless all such people with some sense!

'I cannot say what is fair and not right,' Arjuna said in an even, modest tone. 'Maybe seeing things just and so is, yes, unfair. Wouldn't you say good and bad traverse this course together? Perhaps you are more accustomed to fairways made of Benares silk. No doubt I am behind the times, but may I call you sweet?' But then, in a more serious manner, he added: 'Now is the time, dear Nicolas, for you to convert this place into your own fair way virtue and fine exhibition ground, as it is all experience anyway.'

'But I do not want this freedom!' cried Nicolas, stating this at some volume. 'Give me the tried and true knowing most everyone enjoys, as I have no desire to change anyone. I have only to adjust for them and things will be made right.'

Nicolas went quiet. But then he added, 'Have you not been telling me since we began that all are kin?' And in his grief more sorrowful words came from him.

With tenderness from a kind heart the old man listened. His gentle consideration of the youth, the luckless warrior here, sympathetically understood his grief to be much like his own when he was young and in the company of his exalted good teacher. At that long ago time, when

Arjuna was shockingly pitted against his own cousins, he remembered how he too had undergone his own personal power crisis.

Now Nicolas had the idea that nothing could lift him above his current state of demurral. He thought also that no one need advise him. As the battle lines had been clearly drawn, it occurred to him not even a police lathicharge could get him to start his play here. At this time the challenge-busting feeling sat inside him as a yogi in near-perfect posture. He looked to his clubs sadly. The clubs remained standing by and idle. This put Nicolas in a fouler, more brooding mood. His sad eyes sought Arjuna's. Nicolas looked on the verge of filing a mercy plea. But excusing this youth, by giving him some sympathy waiver, was not at all what this good teacher was willing to do. And Nicolas saw that.

Tension gripped. The feeling of no intention ruled him. He remained seated in this magnificent outdoor space. Nicolas carried on making remarks inside his mind. This produced repeated good starts for more mental agitation.

Will you be the offender or the offended? Nicolas asked his upset self. No, he answered and his gloom darkened. While using his guile he added, I will be neither the offender nor the offended.

6 | *The Unbegun*

Nicolas showed his firm intention. Still, he had a look on his sad face that reached this elder soft as a baby's touch. And the message was that he, Nicolas Kumar, the Unbegun, would be spending an infinite amount of chill time at this spot.

Arjuna smiled. He knew the difficulty in understanding this high philosophy. The old man was not upset, nor was he at all troubled by this refusal. He felt gratified only, thinking mildly, This is the way it is.

He eased back inside his mind. His eyes went more remote. The old man returned to his own formative years. He threw more light onto his distant playing past. The one with the lifelong adolescent smile had returned to his earlier playing self. The young Arjuna was again in the company of his own teacher. This good guide stood all but solidly beside him, plain as day. This life tutor was again instructing him in the most high-ranking way, and the message was that he must go out into this world to perform.

The old man came back to this valley when he felt more in favour of fighting today's battles than yesterday's. All was not lost, however, as Arjuna had brought back with him one nugget of advice.

'Hardest of all and by a long shot,' he said, 'is the going out after the battle, to carry on correctly, while struggling to live daily by these high ideals, and not fall back too often.'

Arjuna wished to press on hard then. He sought to give his youth-rendered philosophics a more serious twirl.

'There are no graves here,' he added. 'Eliminate this first mistake. Take time to understand this, and years may not do, but come to know its verity. Remember, all alive will live always and never have you not been, and nature, while rewarding action, allots little to indifference.'

Arjuna went quiet. He appeared to be formulating what next to say. Then he was back at it, instructing in the fine art of enlightening.

'Now is the time for you to show your great talents,' the old man said, 'being as they are reputed, and to discover a true happiness that is already yours. You are young. Know inexperience as opportunity and nothing to fear. So think well here, dear Nicolas. Come up in life and not down in spirit as performing task is your great instinct.'

Nicolas Kumar refused to budge. Without hint of tiredness, or perceived disappointment, Arjuna contentedly continued.

'Nothing can be achieved without drive,' the old man said, 'and fairest best is the achiever. With your ambitiond, exciting changes will happen to you. So do act, Nicolas, if it wills you. Remember, on this day as with most all others there is need for action.'

Nicolas lifted his eyes to the soaring Indian Himalayas. He thought little of Arjuna's say of words. He felt pushed into this brooding mood. He began hatching a marvelous plan. When Nicolas had more or less worked it out, he shot back with more lip sympathy.

'I am aware of this yet my troubles are not ended. The ball is tiny and from my view the target is small and far off. Can we not just bypass this colourful patch?'

No answer came. A long pause between them ensued. The talking break seemed to chill even the quite cool air.

Nicolas planned to say not one thing more. He told himself it would not be him who spoke first. But then he did so.

'Is it not preferable to forgo play here than to harm these many flowers?' he said. 'Why must I hit into this trouble? What is the purpose served in using this brute force? How could this possibly lead me to get better?'

Nicolas Kumar surveyed a cruel landscape. In an ultimate do-nothing show, he held his breath that lasted upwards of half a minute. He discovered this one life responsibility was difficult to deny. With relief, Nicolas started in again with the activity known as simple breathing.

For a time Arjuna remained silent. He needed this break, between added talk, to think up ways to answer the youth's many-posed questions. He wanted to reassess his approach also, along with his tone. Once Arjuna had worked it out, he returned to instructing though more gently.

'Dear Nicolas' he said. 'Shake off half-heartedness and do the needful. The feeling of enjoy wants to go in: in study, in work, in society from which you take as well as give back. Go into your faith as well as you go into these high hills stuffed to capacity with outstanding history. Go into this happy-sad world and find your own way to create. It will not come to you naturally. This burden comes to you now as a blessing as well as a curse. And the meaning of enjoy is to go out into this world to create and give back joyfully, for yourself and for others, along with for All That Is.'

Throughout, Nicolas Kumar sat with his head downcast. At this time the thought of not playing weighed heavily on him. When he felt sure that the old man was done speaking, he looked up from his sorry low position. He affixed sad eyes on this good teacher.

'Is it because I am afraid?' he asked.

'It is not only this,' answered Arjuna, continuing now in his limitless compassion. 'What is more you have done well in this form science. But science is a friendly shepherd dog wearing spiked collar to discourage hungry, truth-seeking leopards. This is my thinking anyway. What is more too are fear's opposites, love and truth. Science is not love, can it then be truth? Truth is we have life. That is truth. And truth is we will die. The voice will not. The soul and the voice are the same to me. They have a kind of vibration. So when you are talking the voice leaves the body in the shape of the breath and it is all there, your thoughts, what you have been doing, and what you say. That is why it is important to take good care of the words you use because they are you. Of course truth too is this: the equal equation of saying and doing and all you have been thinking.'

The old man went quiet. He allowed a moment to pass in absolute silence. Then he said, 'What is in your past is done now. Your previous thoughts, your words, your actions, all have a life of their own. So you may leave them now or visit some time as you wish.'

Feeling hemmed in, Nicolas Kumar looked away from this good teacher. His mind went on another rampage. He still had serious suspicions over playing up here. His eyes searched all round as a cornered animal's.

Nicolas looked to the striking blue skies for what he held most sacred. Quiet in him returned. He next put together his palms at the chest. He mumbled an oft-recited prayer. The youth hoped that this act of penance might get stamped as recorded in the afterworld, for use in his future help.

'Sending this prayer out into the world is all well and good,' said Arjuna, jumping in at another opportunity to inform. 'But do you have the expectation that something will be done by it?'

The youth's mood brightened. As he had a ready-steady answer for this, his feelings achieved uplift. His sagging spirits rose to new heights. His expression too changed, for the noticeable better. He felt his future remarks would surely rehabilitate him.

Nicolas got even more keyed up. It felt like cheer time.

The human heart is made of human flesh, he recited inside, as some type of preparation. And prayer is what the mind makes up, which comes from the heart.

Nicolas considered this while remaining still seated. He felt certain his forthcoming remarks could bring him back from this hard edge. He believed his future comment might grant him full recovery. Due to his teacher's words, he seemed set again to soar. His only giveaway was a crafty sly smile that was almost indiscernible.

Nicolas Kumar paused as if deep in thought. He shared this moment with God. Then, in a tick, as if he could not hold it in any longer, he was ready to pounce back with the correct quote.

'Well I do,' he said, attempting to hide his glee. 'While I do not pray for someone to come save me, I hope the Goddess Mother would see me as sincere and reap blessings, yes.'

'Hope is a vanity,' said Arjuna, admonishing the youth gently for his earnest appeal.

A moment of some silence stood squarely between them as an eerie phantom. Tension rose. In the core of this, Arjuna wished to change the subject. He thought to say a pleasant morning walk, or taking regular exercise was better than accepting the best help from some one other, meaning mostly himself. Still, he remained quiet. More time passed before Arjuna set out to break the disturbing calm.

'Used as expectation,' he said, 'hope becomes a mode only for spiritual ignorance, clouding what is otherwise a clear-blue sky.'

Nicolas looked to the sky described. He gazed next at this fantastic bowl of land that was cushion-like. He peered out at the valley lit ablaze with bright colour. He felt dazed and deflated. Nicolas seemed under the spell of harsh diseases. He appeared at sea over what to do next. With no sign yet of correct culture to guide him, his heart sank more.

But then he did do something.

Abruptly, Nicolas stood up from his grassy throne. The new entrant to this flowerful arena stepped off the tee-block square without uttering a solitary word. Nicolas strode down to the rushing water. He walked briskly as well as forthrightly down to the fast-flowing stream. He had on a look of defiance in performing some duty.

7 | *The Darker Twin*

At the water's edge the youth saw a small signboard. It was bolted to a vile stake stuck firmly, though savagely into the given green ground, as if on the front lawn of someone's placid-looking home reading: *Test your manhood some other way than by shooting at harmless birds, plants, and animals!*

The 17-year-old youth, with not much hope left, bent down at the limited unclaimed property, or slight clearing by the shimmering blue stream, and kept on edge. The school-going teenager was then on his knees in the peculiar palms' pose that had him looking as one large animal the sign had only just cautioned. From this brute-beast position, living life would be only to find prey, breed, then settle down out here somewhere for the nights.

After the swift parking of his hands, onto the grassy floor, he went further forward as far as he could without tumbling in. Nicolas leaned over where there was a meditative pool of water to look into.

On arriving at this auspicious place, he was nearly prostrate before settling back some. He took a long collected look at the being floating there beneath him. It lay face up in the shallows. It immediately sent back its side of the picture: an effigy on the spot. Laid bare to him there, and appearing to await his warm embrace, was his ghostly darker twin for which he had a twinge of dislike. Curiously, he saw himself as a threat. But then the look on his face grew into an ever-widening gyro, from a dropped bead of sweat off his brow.

This water picture appeared to seek out wildly then a spot far from this centre. The image looked to be fleeing in fear for its own individual safety. The stream returned then to being a nourishing fluidity at ease.

Nicolas reflected well upon his beauty self. He gazed at this personality in the water that was not an uncommon affair. He volunteered to take a long learning look to determine its genuineness more. The pooling water then became a stall only for his undemanding preening needs.

Soon after the meeting of the eyes, Nicolas reached in to take a sip from this mountain stream and supreme beverage of choice to anyone. He put in his big dippers as if offering hard cash at the temple to ensure the best result. The youth watched the water cram onto his hands in an apparent bid to make its own surreptitious escape. Nicolas looked to the stream's centre. He felt the water was a lot like him at this time, preferring lower places as being far more appropriate.

He perceived a host of flowers on that far side of the stream. They appeared wrapped in bundles for making commendable gifts. But then the variety of wildflowers on that far side made for a less-pleasing sensation. Again, he gazed down at the water where like splendour had been written. He was absorbed by this, his gorgeousness self, or fave hero in apparent good health, depicted just then at a sort of side profile. He smiled.

Nicolas looked away from his own eyes as if unable to bear modeling more. At next glance the familiar image, or case of ego clash appeared oddly to calm him. He moved to take a superb drink. Nicolas reached in again with cupped hands to touch the most startling texture ever. His thoughts too wandered. They fled from thinking of playing on this high course with little hope of reward. His mind went away from the terrible task of performing here, for the O so simple reason that it could.

He concentrated on the water. Nicolas discovered as from out of the blue he was no longer eager to resist more. This look seemed supported by a blue sky riding pillion. The water did not suggest any option for him, other than to go on and start his play up here.

Nicolas considered the eternal question of getting out there and performing. Relating to this sensation, greater intensity crept. He thought it was not too unreasonable now to step onto this flower community. He felt all might be okay. But in another attempt at prolonging, the words 'Be professional and polite' came to bless and pass by his lips.

He mustered courage then stood up. Back on the ground, after multiple stares down in the water, along with staring down some his own myths, the bottoms of his feet stamped down hard all calls over leaving here. And for a moment he lost all interest in this place: the ongoing coordination from all in the outdoors, seemingly hell-bent on grinding at him in bombastic opposition.

Nicolas returned then from this distance a species standing. He was a pulsating, upright form now walking but with the renewed powers of reasoning. The youth or undertrial, his mind in the active state and feeling charged at this hour, ruled out all calls for reassessing. He scanned the flowers of sizable number. He estimated their near-total destruction.

As for explaining his departure to the middling stream, he broke through all cordons. Nicolas Kumar thought to say to this awaiting teacher, I am ready now. Then he did so. He arrived back on the tee-block square and he looked to Arjuna. Without caution or more concern-for-all hesitation he said, 'I’m ready now,' and he felt the tiny stings and tingles of a hundred thousand million eyes pierce onto him.

Arjuna showed his famous grin. His trademarked boyhood beam was a mix of fun and jest. His gladness seemed as all in the outside world: doing rather well at this time and was also quite spacious. It was an occasion of sheer happiness to him. His smile could be seen too, the youth thought, as a gateway to some quite cool resilience.

The old man's cheerfulness was a surprise to the youth. He had anticipated a thorough top-to-bottom chastising by him for having stormed off the mound that way.

For his part, Arjuna was glad the youth had, all by himself, removed his opposition on playing here. He felt pleased too from the beauty thought he was having from the old song stating even the longest journey begins with a solitary step.

Arjuna's happiness was such he might have declared four days of celebration. However, in keeping with tradition, by attempting to set up some spiritual end, he did not set out to burst like firecrackers. Instead, the old man went to pick up the transcendental conch that was beside his small pack. Soon he had in his hands the overlarge *devadatta,* or great battle-shell that was Lord Indra's loud gift.

The old man came back smiling. He looked as if he wanted to exchange a few jokes. He went to put a hand on the youth's right shoulder. Arjuna appeared ready to tell him he had been part of a practical joke. Smiling, holding something back, the old man looked as if he were going to say that he had all along been part of some half-comic reality show, or nutty TV promo, set up to trap him. But Arjuna told not one thing about any joke. He said only, and with some understatement, 'Very well, then.' And, 'If you insist.'

Arjuna stepped back a pace. He set then about fiddling with the conch by raising the shell with both hands. He looked as if he were about to play a jazzy tune on a saxophone. The old man's thoughts too ranged, as he fingered the age-old horn. Arjuna wished not to allow what was meant only as a brief observance to be blown out of all proportion.

Several seconds passed as he tried finding a good grip. His idea to get Nicolas to start his play here seemed to hang in the balance. Time ticked. The beating heart of the watcher ticked away. Nicolas Kumar put his hands on his hips in the western aggressive manner. He questioned from impatience whether this good teacher was capable of doing whatever it was he was trying to do.

But then Arjuna did find good grip. He lowered then raised sharply the conch to his lips. He took in a breath to fill up his lungs. The trumpet seashell, or great attribute to Vishnu that was remarkably found in these high mountains, and so was measureless years old, sounded loud over the Valley of Flowers. It resonated over this high hill district especially blessed by Lord Brahma. The old man blew the instrument with the sweetest strain that might have covered miles. The musical device of primal energy, which traditionally signals the start of play anywhere, could again be heard. The old man sounded the horn across this many-flowered valley, or outstanding setting for creating perfect legends.

Louder still, Arjuna put out the call to all youth everywhere to get out there and perform.

The old man lowered the conch for keeps. He headed to the rear of the tee box. He returned the ancient sea-born noise producer. On coming back, Arjuna removed his shawl worn on this somewhat chilly morning. He perceived his younger more proud-playing self. Arjuna went between being young and then old without having much preference. The old man removed his jacket. He went over as a warrior might to the youth's standing pack.

As for the clubs, they looked almost bored. They stood at military attention in the off chance they might be needed.

Arjuna shifted the irons around to simply hear their sound. He rested a hand on the driver. He stood there thinking for a moment. The old man stared at the many-flowered valley. He asked for and received one ball.

The youth handed him also one red tee. Arjuna removed the cover of the driver. He yanked the club out from the youth's standing pack. He went to set the ball atop the tee or position-holder. The old man backed up step by slow step. He stopped a few paces behind the ball, and here his expression changed. Arjuna went from appearing friendly to one familiar with being quite fierce. He seemed used to severe brooding. The old man looked ready to stare down this flower fairway forever.

Arjuna next made a few arm movements loosely associated with helpful stretching. He stood the driver against himself. He extended an arm over his head while his other arm went behind his back where his two hands clasped. He looked to be turning himself into a twisted salted pretzel.

He gauged the length of one spot to hit his drive. The place he had in mind was sparked by the sun burning bright. As with the one lit ablaze, that splendid moving luminary, all in the valley appeared filled with limitless fresh beginnings. Arjuna returned to a scene that had happened long ago. He looked light-years away. The old man arrived as if on time to witness again the very moment he had shown his playing skills so well. The young-again Arjuna was back then, at that prestigious tourney, set so deep in his past though not forgotten. Now any would believe a miraculous event was about to take place.

8 | *The One Called King*

Arjuna was then in full flashback mode. He flitted between this one reality as well as all abstract time with the seeming joy of a boy. He arrived fighting fit in both arenas, referred to by life practitioners as then and now. The old man threw in plenty of crowd sounds to go with his imagining. Arjuna recalled the virulent hand claps he had always received in his day. The large crowd shouted now from all four grand directional points of the compass save one. They cheered him on wildly as their valiant hero.

Arjuna's army, three bands fifty and he at the helm as their brigade commander, was back again. The gambling rebel in him too had returned, and with plenty of time on his hands.

The one with the great charisma recalled the thunderous applause he had always received from his once-magnificent army. This resounded deafeningly now in his ears. Arjuna's mind had only just come back to the valley when a gigantic roar lit up over one section of this fantastic flower crowd.

The old man watched himself as in real-time video. Arjuna saw his younger self bend low to tee up on the opening hole of his first major. He recalled a day earlier at practise when a pair of two well-known players, both in mid-careers at the time, and where one afforded him a challenge-promoting comment. The remark had at first mortified him. Later, as the days turned into months then years that too piled up, the words only gladdened him. He felt this moment had helped shape him as a player as well as into a mature man. The comment added greatly to his cherished memories of the yesteryears.

The incident took place when one of the pair of marquee names, considered today among the game's battle-hardened legends, grimaced while watching Arjuna take yet another nervous hack at the ball. This famous player said to the other, and loud enough that Arjuna can hear it, 'What is this kid doing here?'

Another recollection came to him. He recalled with warm fondness the satisfied look on the venerable man himself. Arjuna remembered having recognised instantly the grand master of this celebrated tourney. The great gentleman was in his chair at the time and smiling. He looked as if he were enjoying a well-earned breather. He seemed to welcome this tough brand of mental competition.

In utterless awe, Arjuna thought it remarkable that this one man is voted, even in this modern day and age, time after time still, as the greatest player who ever lived. He returned then to this many-flowered valley, surrounded by glittering tranquil palaces, designed by some unperceived greatness.

A picture appeared of this famous player. It showed in the sky near one mountain peak. It was near the heavens also. The black & white image, a smiling, handsome young man, looking out from the past, seemed to have been taken at the time of his greatest triumph: achieving golf's Grand Slam.

The image Arjuna had in mind was the size of a building's hoarding. It appeared to entice all who might try their luck here with the message, *Come relax with the Divine*. Flash forward to today, on a superb bright-lit summer's morning, the message rumbled with authority.

Arjuna's consciousness came back to register one practise swing. He understood the decision to swing had been made on his behalf while he was away. He wanted to know how this could happen without him being properly informed.

His fidgety reflexes perked up then. He gripped the upstart driver in an effort to quell a rebellion. The youthful Arjuna, with the down-to-earth manner, appeared ready to take up the big swing. He looked all set to go with his flamboyant go-for style that was all out. His body went through a flurry of whipped-up activities when another practise swing was administered and this time he was present.

The swing was a genial leg-spinner. It seemed sweetened for any situational humour on prime time TV. It was over in a flash when the club rose up at the follow through in apparent high triumph.

Arjuna remained pointing towards the heavens. His follow through appeared to be a solemn flag-hoist. This seemed to be one for the guys. He rested the club onto his shoulder to the memory of those he was fond of recalling. In his heart he knew that they were temporarily inhabiting the grandest of all pasturelands, to get refreshed, before coming back to compete again, with an equal amount of style, along with a whole lot of grace.

With his feet somewhat planted, he hitched up his pants. He did this a time or two more, in a routine that could pass as a ritual in some pagan religion. His pants seemed in urgent need of alteration. This was quite entertaining to the youth. Nicolas looked to have benefited immensely. He thought it rather curious to get ready this way, one in which nobody could forget soon.

The once-assured, or one called King by his legion of loyal followers, and begrudgingly so by his former competitors, turned his hips to stand better over the ball. The old man backed away from it. He stepped out of the pocket to walk a few paces behind. Arjuna gave the ball and fairway a long look. He did this while furiously reforming his grip on the driver. A moment passed before the old man went back into it. Arjuna had a look on his face that could scare crows.

He stepped up. Arjuna took his stance over a ball that he perceived as being somewhat intimidated by him. Man and ball then gave one another a wink-wink knowingness over who was really and truly the boss up here. This stare-down left one participant a tad undecided. After which, that one backed off.

Again, Arjuna stepped away from the plate to take several quarter-swings. The stern look on his face, along with the sorrowful shaking of his head, appeared to suggest that stepping away was indeed needed.

The young-again Arjuna came back into it. He settled back into his stance. When he seemed more or less persuaded by it, a waft of wind arrived to thwart him. The wind came in again to antagonise more.

The youth gave no thought to the breeze. He was concerned only with the swing of this past master. The chill air calmed. It moved Arjuna to arrive at some acceptance. Soon he was a mere dot presence in the glory of All. No friend, the wind kicked up again to chide him.

Nicolas was glad to not be the one at the plate at this time. He heaved a sigh of relief that it would not be him teeing off there and then. For the moment, he was happy not to be the one getting that kind of unwanted wind attention.

Arjuna backed off again to take more practise swings. The twisted set of body instructions that followed seemed not to be coming from an otherwise sane man. To the uninitiated, Arjuna's swing might have looked like it had come up from one or more layers of Dante's hell.

It occurred to Nicolas the old man's swing, known at one time as The End-bringer, could not have been manifested from the known world. To him, Arjuna's swing seemed to be an odd dance mix of hop, tap, bop, with a bit of boogie thrown in.

But then his swing did change. It had acquired a finer, more poetic line.

Indeed, Arjuna's swing no longer seemed to be punishing some wayward sinner.

Still, he finished hands-up high as if caught in a crime.

A breeze came in to open the youth's shutters to an altered way of seeing. Strong wisps arrived as if to say Arjuna's swing was a thing that he might cherish. Next thing Nicolas heard his mind say was that he should appreciate all things. This included, he assumed, was the old man's twisting up follow through.

Arjuna wailed away at another practise swing. The club had hit the ground hard at impact. This offered up yet another thing to love called turf. The fantastic god-creation known as Arjuna's swing went wild yet again. Gladly it seemed his swing had finished arms, elbows, along with hands-up high. A changed man, Nicolas now saw the old man's swing as a thing of utmost beauty.

One more blow came down on the Earth heavy. The turf that rose seemed to pop up and ask, *Why me?* In place of genuine kindness, Nicolas felt the breeze had meant for him to be more honest. This may have resulted in him coughing up a lung from laughter.

Again, the youth heard inside his head the call to accept all swing gyrations. Nicolas heard his mind say, These too are born and created things. It meant each was lovely, a thing to cherish and not scoff at. But then he looked at Arjuna's swing that appeared to be a series of extreme wrongdoings. Nicolas Kumar wanted to know how something as beautiful and natural as a golf swing could go so wrong.

As he did not want to be detected for any sniper grinning, his head shot back down to stare at a patch of grass that had become so exceedingly interesting. He placed his forefinger and thumb under his chin. Nicolas thought to assume the guise of a practising philosopher.

From this down-looking position, he heard another swing fly by. Nicolas Kumar stifled another smirk. He suffocated it sufficiently. He was hard at work inventing an expression that he could show more publicly. He returned to observing the old man's efforts at getting started up here.

After more practise swings, Arjuna yet again backed off his three-point stance. He appeared to step away from the plate to escape some undetermined pressure.

The old man took in more of the valley. He studied all he surveyed. He smiled. He peered at the Indian Himalayas that looked made up of vanilla ice cream. The upturned cones with ice cream on top were vast and majestic. They seemed moderately eaten also from a few bright-lit days.

Often, especially on days when cotton candy seemed to fill the skies, he thought of those residing up in the heavenly beyond. Without a word, the old man stepped towards the one teed up. He went step by slow step towards the one that had previously stung his soul. He went as one attempting to get back his swag or say-so.

Nicolas sent his head back down. He studied once more the patch of grass that had so fascinated him. He feared what may come from the old man's sudden moves at the ball. He hid yet another urge to crack up.

One question loomed in the gloom and seemed destined to remain beyond his efforts at mind control. The idea crept close and stayed. It had parked there in his little bean. The suggestion seemed as if it may remain until someone brave happened along to tell Arjuna a thing or two about the ease of hitting a little white ball, which was not even moving.

The old man took another turn at things. This induced one more gash in the ground. A gash too showed on the youth's now-hurting face. Nicolas saw another clump of grass pop up. It looked like a newly awoken visitor. The grass seemed determined to relate a grievance to some park ranger.

Arjuna's next swing saw more grass pop up to complain. A chunk flew off to one area. It appeared to look for outside help. Arjuna's slashing at the ground opened up something more. The youth may have suffered an even wider grin had his hand not reached up just then to save the day. Nicolas was glad the old man had not turned and looked his way.

In place of finding out, Arjuna had discovered a good grip. Yet even this required evermore adjustments.

A familiar query arrived in the youth's mind. It swirled as if carried on the wind. The thought suggested that he give up his quest for overall fairness. His mind seemed to be telling him to quit his claim that all should be deemed lovely.

Yet another question could be heard in the remote regions of his mind. The idea pushed forward. Nicolas wanted to say aloud what he would only dare muster under his breath. Both breeze and boy confided in one another. Rebellion brewed within the ranks. Together, in the youth's outgoing breath, the two, acting like juvenile delinquents, managed to say in unison, faint but not vaguely, 'Could that swing have ever actually worked?'

9 | *A Memorable Head-to-Head*

Nicolas Kumar concerned himself next with the old man's hand and arm movements. He felt they were far too hurried. He believed there were needless gestures in them for such a task as easy as hitting a little white ball.

As with the clubs, the one teed-up looked almost bored. It appeared fed up with all the swing practise and dealt with it simply by ignoring it. The ball seemed to be in a state it had always been in: looking rather relaxed with who and what it was at this time, while waiting for someone other to get his act together.

To Arjuna, the ball remained parked atop the tee as a glamourised person. It sat fat on its sleek red throne. It had the look of a hot-shot celebrity pro, accustomed to being catered to. In comparison to Arjuna, the ball looked markedly composed. It appeared to not have one worldly care. The look on the old man's face, however, suggested the ball had, as if by magic, become something of a soothe-saying mystic. It occurred to him that the ball could, in the next instant, start levitating.

Arjuna's focus switched up. He went from being somewhat interested in the ball to all-out hypnotic. He had on a look of disbelief. Arjuna appeared incredulous as to how the ball could outdo him in the matter of mind control.

Concerning the old man's stance, Nicolas thought it was a bit askew. To him it seemed he was aiming left towards the tribal regions of Pakistan. The clubhead, on the other hand, appeared to have altogether different travel plans. It looked to be heading right in the general direction of Kathmandu. The old man's set up seemed hell bent on dying a miserable death.

It’s a stance and swing worthy of a few giggles, he thought.

Next he went back to considering the old man's everlasting requirement to shift about so. He felt Arjuna need not mess with his grip so often. What really is the point in all that?

As if he had heard, Arjuna left off the agreement or mafia goon contract he seemingly had out on the grip. He let go some his hold on the grip or one nearly strangled to give his trousers a hike. Still unsure about hitting the old man went at his pants as a seamstress might in taking up the slack. He gave his pants a quick tug, one side then the other, as if this would set things right or situate positive all that made life wretched in this world: hunger, poverty, disease.

When he appeared to have settled the matter with his pants, though issues still remained, Arjuna viewed with equal eye the eternal restlessness of all in the Valley of Flowers. He stared out at this wild that went on serenely. The old man added a few half-practise swings for no real good reason.

'He might cut down on his pace,' said Nicolas softly, so no one could hear. Yes, that would be one thing he could do, agreed another inside. 'Among many,' chimed in the first, in a voice nobody could possibly catch. He’s doing his best as coach or life guide, said the second from within. But he cannot be expected to do everything. Nicolas told himself also, Well it is true he is good with his life-fielding drills. He is good with his life strategies too, said this one who made the other stay quiet inside. Of this there is no smidgen of doubt. But he cannot be expected to do everything.

Arjuna focused on an area two hundred meters or so out. He viewed his chosen landing spot on the flowered fairway. He stood ready to make an attempt at it by not thinking too much. He had always believed it was best to simply step up, concentrate on a colour, an ocean-blue maybe, then swing all out. Nevertheless, Arjuna understood once age catches up with any morning walker he is put back more times than he gets going forward. With this knowing gift, the old man smiled at his current predicament. He became happy, fully aware where he was now physically and from how amusing this must seem to all those standing by waiting patiently.

To combat his known deficits more, the old man thought to breathe in deep and just relax. The value of the breath or simple breathing is greatly underrated, considered Arjuna. He thought how much he enjoyed being in the mountains or accumulation of centuries. He was happiest, he well knew, being up in the glorious untamed. He felt glad too being in the company of this fine young fellow.

The old man understood well that while held in by age, in the immediate present, he was free to travel back in his past and do so whenever he liked. Though he had yearnings for his drive to attain good height, length, then have it sit up nicely on some turf, he knew it might not happen that way and he was content with that. In performing any life duty, the old man thought it well and good to intellectually plan it first, but then be willing to let go of the intellect, to carry on intuitively, to allow any idea to develop and live as it might. He thought this ideal for his stage in life known as the *sannyasi* or one in full retirement.

Arjuna felt it was best to use his powers of letting go. He believed the intellect, or splendid mind gift should be used selectively. He remembered then welcomed the glad return of his younger playing self. Arjuna became one character in three places without divisions. One looked to have arrived from that long ago major battlefield. This one stood by silently. To get ready more, the old man evoked the three breathings: *prana*, *vyana*, *apana*. This exercise gives all who try it their ultimate strength in performing an endeavour. Arjuna concentrated on this ancient technique in proper breathing. With clearness and directness of thought, he remained quiet.

Keep the peace and do not go looking for more excitement, he advised his younger self. This was meant to relax him so he might calmly enjoy the essence. But then a cleanliness drive was started by him.

Originally, when Arjuna first set out for Europe, then onto America to play golf professionally, this routine had begun in fun; however, it soon became a psychic need. Mental fret morphed into all-out physical fuss. Then it went permanent.

On the 1st tee of this Himalayan course known as Truind, the old man's energy, based somewhat on fear and anxiety, began covering both forearms and pant legs. His free hand went to wipe the face of the silver clubhead. The old man did this in repeated fast motion. Arjuna's hand rose to wipe a bit of sweat off his forehead. In another incarnation of fearing, Arjuna moistened his left thumb that wiped again the face of the silver-headed driver. That done, he brushed his cheeks with two fingers. He wiped below the nose. This act went to his forehead to swab what wetness was retained. With his hand acting on fear's behalf, the old man moved to brush down the puff clouds he had for hair. His hand stayed to pat down all on top. A breeze passed for no reason, other than to mess with his crowning achievements.

The old man went about correcting what had been undone. He did this in a flash. Arjuna had made his hand work as a four-fingered comb. His hand acted also as a kind of towel tool. It helped erase any lingering wetness. His hand next made the trip down with his hard-at-work fingers to pluck a time or two at the shoulders' area. Arjuna pulled again at his shirt to be extra certain. In this way he hoped his arms, shoulders, his armpits too, could get more breathing room.

Purity achieved, Arjuna negotiated another safe spot for his tee shot to land.

He looked ready now to put in motion the final touches of yet one more club waggle. Nicolas felt he did this to avoid the actual hitting of the little white ball. How easy can it be! he shouted in his head. The thing's not even moving!

Another practise swing occurred for no real reason. Nicolas cleared his throat. He wished to clear the air also by saying a thing or two about Arjuna's inability to get things rolling. Inside the youth cried out, Why not just hit the thing!

Following more grip renewals, a focused calm appeared on the one with the apparent heavy burden. It may have looked to all and sundry that Arjuna was about ready to hit, and do so with a bit of oomph.

After all the obsessions over his clothes, his stance, grip, the clubhead, his face and hair also, at no other time before now did the old man appear ready to do what was required. And what was asked was that he strike the little white ball and end this sordid drama.

The old man gazed out at the flower fairway while Nicolas held back another smile. In place of actually beaming, the youth again sought the grass for some serious mental help.

Arjuna shifted. He wiggled his hips to settle in better or add more comedy to this outdoor amphitheater. Arjuna took the driver back. It returned to its original starting point looking rather reluctant. The club went back to its apparent rightful position, stuck behind a little white ball.

The old man's focus was again on this round ruler atop the tee. Arjuna saw the ball as his equal counterpart in this epic drama by Homer. With corded muscles, he seemed so fixed he appeared catatonic. This was followed fast by a glance down the flower fairway as if one contestant had blinked in a stare fight. He fretted being thought of as soft on rotund little criminals. Arjuna feared being pelted by stones also, if he did not take the shot soon. He looked at the ground as the two sides of his brain quarreled. They seemed unable to agree on what to do next.

An abbreviated club waggle brought the old man's focus back onto the club then that was still stuck behind the little white ball. The club held up above the moist ground. His club looked to be performing the sideshow trick known as yogic levitation.

Except for scattered here and there chatter, blown in on a breeze, the Valley of Flowers was an area of perfect peace and silence.

The old man's mind also arrived at a place of some peace. Stillness overcame him. Quiet too came to his vast army of followers with the countless crossed fingers. All seemed well and about to get going when Arjuna's one remaining grouse was the actual hitting of the little white ball.

He hesitated more. Arjuna thought to study a few film clips from his former playing days. He soon gave that up though. He came in as from out of the cold to the surprise of at least one, himself. More surprise too was in store for him when he noticed that the club was now inching back.

At first he could not believe what his eyes were telling him. But then he saw the driver was indeed extending rearward. It moved along a straight line and in earnest this time. The club travelled low and slow. Its silver coating made it seem like a snow leopard stalking. The sleek beast crept across the moist grass slowly. It left a visible trail where dew had been. The club was lifted up sharply. His hips turned from the tension caused by his also-turning shoulders. The club arrived at a spot short of its usual preparatory high point in any swing's life, which was at parallel. The old man looked determined now to haul off and belt it.

In the next instant, the young-again Arjuna threw life off to death and let life be born to it yet again and the ball was away, itself a born and created thing. The one flying, rising majestic and beautiful, took its rightful spot up among the gods in heaven. It seemed content in that high place.

Arjuna had finished on a high as well. He had ended with his trademarked flying-high elbows. To those looking on anxiously, the club pointing up may have appeared to be a spiraling-up staircase. His finish seemed to be showing a direct path to the high holy gates. To others, Arjuna might have looked as if he were holding a sword, beckoning all comers to try and test him. It only ended for him with the sudden realisation that this psychic trauma was now over.

He stayed in this follow through position. Arjuna remained posed or beautifully suspended. He felt that the youth could benefit from this awesome display of power. He wanted to make certain a lesson had indeed been learned.

Then the moment came when all had time enough to study his swing and take good note. The old man brought the club down. He laid it onto his left shoulder. He did this, but not before allowing photographers their time needed to record, for tomorrow's headlines say, this memorable head-to-head.

10 | *A Collective Trousers-Hike*

Back onto this hard-matter existence, curiously referred to as a type of present, Arjuna had bowled a googly. In this one reality, hard and physical, the old man had hit a Jerry Ford crowd-ducker into the first shoots of flowers. He had sclaffed the ground hard at impact and the ball left the tee lead-like. It looked shot from a country-made pistol. It had taken off in what is commonly termed as plain ugly.

The ball had gone stem-skimming. It had ignored the lake or problem area referred to astutely by game regulators as a water hazard. The ball had appeared to search hastily for a reasonable spot to exit. This was in contrast to its earlier incarnation back on the tee as one cool customer. The ball had scurried off in the sidelined marginalia as a vacationist. It went into an area not too far off the mound. It had gone into a place where it looked like hay was kept.

Arjuna's swing finished high. His arms twisted up in his trademarked corkscrew. He had on an expression that was a true collector's item. He looked to where his ball had gone with a mixture of relief and some stark disbelief. Arjuna understood now it had gone in a nearby maze of flowers to perhaps live in the company of gods. His drive had fallen far short of his high hopes for it. The old man called after the shot then with renewed gusto.

'Ball, may you reincarnate as a two-toed, pod-shod Gujarati camel!' he said.

With clenched fist held quaking near his mouth, the youth resisted laughing outright. But then a large smile did break through. His grin showed where before it had been strictly forbidden.

The old man smiled too. He understood well the precarious nature of participating on this hard plane of existence. He was filled then with the feeling of outright humility.

Nicolas Kumar broke loose. He burst out laughing without much regard for how it might be perceived outwardly.

Arjuna turned to him. The old man said in mock-apology, for his comment over a well-known ornery Indian camel, 'Forgive me, friend.'

Arjuna took this chance to play-act more. He did it for the youth's enjoyment, as well as for his ever-present vast army.

The old man returned the clubhead to the ground. He did this in a resigning gesture. He shook his head in performed disbelief. He went on to his act's next logical conclusion. He tapped down the ground that had strangely popped up. He knocked back the dreaming tufts of grass. The old man followed this with his brand of humour, over a ball that had clearly gone missing.

'Is it gone?' he cracked, and the youth laughed until a flow of tears came to make him stop.

'Yeah,' Nicolas managed, adding the needless.

Arjuna stepped forward once. His pant leg was given one final hike, as if this was the thing missing from his earlier preparations. This was followed fast by a deep-knee bend.

The old man swiped across the grass with his one free hand. He picked up the remains of the tee. He flicked the mortally wounded thing off to the side with performed disdain. He looked to the youth for added confirmation that all was well and good up here and smiled.

Nicolas went along gladly with the old man. He laughed while appearing to cry also. The old man’s infectious smile, along with the youth’s own good humour, turned each to enjoying life with laughter. Both shrugged. But then, what came to the youth next was the sudden realisation it was his turn to play. Nicolas understood the moment to start his play here, in India's northern reaches, had just now arrived.

Inside the fright sense came to him then as butterflies in the thousands. This tryst with the terror feeling did not come alone. What came to greet him next, as to thrust him hard under a glaring spotlight, was the urgent but not unexpected need to find a place up here, in these wide-open spaces, to privately pee.

Nicolas Kumar went to relieve himself. On coming back he discovered that his mind had gone missing. This seemed to be not enough to the gods hell bent on messing with him, as the wind picked up just then as if to toss him. He pretended he was all bashed up. To him, the flowers had been pulled up and were just now darting him. He imagined that he was made up of pierced metal.

To help himself more, Nicolas focused next on his rucksack that stood by in tacky splendour. He then made the effort to return from wherever his mind had gone. Nicolas thought to take delivery of his own driver. He decided if he were still in this confused state, he could go through the motions and tee off anyway. Nicolas felt he might rely on muscle memory to get through the shot. He believed he could still get rewarded for producing.

Before being handed the driver, Nicolas told himself that he would not take as much time as this elder. His thinker went through another dramatic flight. He had yet another go over the sorry plight of the flowers. His fearing pulled him from his body. This left him so immobile.

Like by magic, he discovered his jacket had miraculously been removed. It lay now atop his clubs in his rucksack. He discovered too that his left hand was reaching out just then for a driver he did not now recognise. Arjuna gave Nicolas the club like nothing at all was wrong. The old man handed the club to him as if it were a common broom and he had in mind a few household chores for him to come do. For his part, Nicolas felt he had been given the sweeping item with no real instructions on how to actually use it.

In his other hand, he discovered one ball and also one tee. The sad look of the tee and ball made them appear headed for some premature end. Nicolas sent out his sight to patrol all in the valley. He looked at those whose only apparent crime was to stand there and look pretty.

Nicolas Kumar looked to the flowers lit ablaze by fantastic hues. He peered out at the sparkling lake. He automatically determined the lake to be within reach. It seemed to be in cahoots with the sky-highs. Nicolas looked from the lake's mountain reflection to other areas in the valley. Included in this were his usual subtle yardstick calculations. He turned his attention next from the fairway and cool air and blazing sunshine to the spectacular waterfall and escalating Indian Himalayas, rising to great heights in the background.

Nicolas returned in his mind to the time of his own greatest glory. Unlike Arjuna, the time he thought of was not too far back. It was only two weeks ago when he had qualified for the Open Championship. With this rediscovery of his great golfing self, he came back and said quietly, 'But how shall I among friends?'

He looked at the fast-flowing stream. He searched for its ever-present tranquility. He hunted next for then found the sign that had attempted to ward off all trespassers. Nicolas peered at the Valley of Flowers that was plagued riotously by colourful wildflowers. His feelings sank into sadness. He fretted again over the fate of these scented little beauties.

Is this designed only to tarnish my name? Nicolas asked his upset self. Nobody should be allowed to malign me.

He tried to relax. Nicolas believed it was best to take it easy. He pulled from his back pocket the course map or journal. Nicolas began reading from it, though not this time for the perceived bit of bad poetry. He read for the actual concrete yard measurements. He looked down at the map for helpful tidbits that could be gleaned from it if any.

One option came to him. The idea was to hit it into the lake. Again Nicolas judged the lake area to be within reach. He thought to hit it to a spot more conventional. The idea of sending his drive into the drink returned to like light him up. Nicolas thought more on the gravity of his sorry situation. He felt hitting it into the lake was the best of bad choices He began calculating the force needed for just such a drive.

Gaining merit here won't be easy, he told himself.

The thought of hitting in the lake shined in him. Nicolas put on a slight smile. He felt he would be saving lives this way.

Yes, he thought. Then he said quietly, 'Easy. Take it easy.'

His considerations included the breeze coming in from the east. It travelled about five kilometres per hour. Nicolas felt its change of direction. It occurred to him this quick-change artist had been sent to aid him. More likely, he well knew, the wind had arrived to plague or even stop him.

Nicolas chose not to oppose the idea of sending his drive in the lake. He felt relieved after deciding. He asked his self if he should use his 3-iron or his 3-wood. One feeling rose suggesting that he use neither. That sense forwarded some. It raced down to his awaiting-production hands that did just that. And the reason his little grippers might have given for the hold up, if able, would have been of the nature-loving kind.

He told himself next, Nothing is ever permanent.

Nicolas went to put his driver back in his pack. He set aside his jacket that lay on top. He then returned the club to his grouped-up set or perceived dud kit. He thought next of his forthcoming offence against life. Nicolas yanked from his pack the 3-wood he called Little Benefit. The club was his chosen candidate to avoid all flower destruction.

His choice appeared final. The expression on his hardened face suggested a landmark judgment had just been handed down from the High Court, after 10 years of waiting.

11 | *The Two-Plank Strategy*

'Here you should not look for shortcuts,' Arjuna advised. 'Nor should you seek ladders to step easily onto some top, as the priority here is to participate. Whether upon peak or fair open valley, you should not be in any mad rush to ape others who have come to this high place.'

The old man took in a breath. He considered what more to add. He said, 'Now is the time to create for yourself, and for All That Is, because at very essence you are alone here.'

Nicolas felt confused. I am alone here? he asked himself. It occurred to him that he might avoid all unnecessary heat by just staying quiet. Nicolas thought to step up and take a whack at it, short and sweet. Yet he was going nowhere. He looked at the ball put up on display. It seemed to be resting atop the tee comfortably. The ball looked like a monument highlighting his own inactivity.

Nicolas needed help saying *Yes!* to it. His mind, however, remained uncertain. He hesitated. The youth could not hit, or cremate this body of a ball until he had received word or gotten the green signal. Nicolas wished to be free of these heavy-as-iron 18 holes, linked each-to-each, which he felt were clasped round his prisoner legs. He looked forward to being free of these manacles.

Nicolas Kumar peered out at the lake. The lake was known to village locals, domestic tourists, the legions of pilgrims who visit barefoot annually as the Protector of the Masses. The Protector of the Masses Lake lay well within range of his trusty 3-wood. He thought once more to consign his tee shot there. Nicolas felt clever thinking he could hit it into the water hazard and therefore waste it.

Still he said aloud, so this good guide could hear it, 'Never have I felt so bad on a course.'

Not one word came back from Arjuna. As Nicolas hoped to come out of this with clean hands, he decided he would send his drive into the lake or catchment area. The youth felt it worthwhile to incur the what-the-hell penalty, and do so whether this good teacher liked it or not.

Yes, I believe I will, he thought, reaffirming his choice, and he pointed down the flower fairway at the sparkling lake.

He told Arjuna, 'As I want *moksha* for myself, I will play for it to go there and hope for divine charity. This is so my soul won't forever be cussing me.'

Arjuna offered nothing by way of a returning comment. It puzzled young Nicolas. He believed this teacher could not possibly be lost for words. He threw Arjuna a glance. He discovered the old man was looking low and that his head was downcast. He saw too that Arjuna was smiling slightly. To Nicolas, the old man seemed to agree with his decision to put it in the lake. But then it occurred to him that Arjuna may have given up altogether on instructing him.

Either way it was no longer in his power to say, he thought. I am going to do it.

As this guide no longer had much stronghold over him, he felt good about his decision. Nicolas stepped a few paces behind the ball to line up. He was enjoying this teacher's solemn silence and he hoped it might continue.

'Only a few measured steps,' Nicolas whispered, and again he stared down the many-flowered fairway.

Stand there and do not think of a solitary thing, the youth said inside. Before taking up the club, think only to set it at the top. Hold it a split second or so. A full swing with not a lot of power will get you there.

Nicolas, done speaking to himself, moved to set up. With his feet somewhat planted, he lowered the clubhead behind the ball. Arjuna coughed. Nicolas looked sharply his way.

'Wonderful!' cried Arjuna. 'Choosing which side to stand is an excellent place to start. You were probably just asking yourself, Shall I take the right-hand path or the left? If you were thinking this, you must know that victory by way of the left is known as the Hero Path. Victory by way of the right is that of the Devotee. Of course there is a third way. This most hallowed path doesn't clamour for the reliability of idolisms or perceived perspectivisms. Nor does it require the staging of oaths that appear to deem, to the mind of the simple, one good. This way can be called The Way of the Celestial. It is neither left nor right nor here nor there. It is of the quiet mind only, seeking out ways to approach the feet of the Mother, and do so with utmost respect. These three are all just and good, of course, as I am not saying they are not. And my saying this is just and good is also choice. I only say this to discourage imparting simplicity or bland discourse. Now I can see on your face by the roll of your eyes I have gone on too much. Please, continue with whatever it was you were doing.'

Nicolas thought the old man's speech somewhat overlong. He considered what all was said but did not catch a whole lot of meaning. He took note of this and told himself also, If even there was any meaning. He thought this guide's interruption gave him an excuse to back off the shot and he decided to accept it.

Nicolas stepped out of the pocket or open beggar's home. He removed himself from the usual set-up position. He did this in the manner Arjuna had done not that long before. He stepped three paces to the rear. Nicolas went to a spot he hoped might provide his refuge. He backed up a fourth step to get away more.

Along the way, he gave this teacher a long look. He peered at Arjuna while pretending to be O so deeply disappointed in him. News came crushingly back then to inform him that it was his turn to play. It warned him over issuing evermore excuses. The choice, Nicolas heard inside his head, is yours.

He looked doomed out over the Valley of Flowers' fairway. Nicolas stood as one who had been ill but had since gotten over it. He looked as if he had been given a blessed second chance. He decided next on one area in the lake to hit. He stepped up with renewed focus. He felt strengthened by his known ability to swing to near-perfection. He approached the round one atop the tee as a devotee visiting Swami.

Back at the ball, he put his right foot forward then the other. He observed a moment of intense devotion. He looked as if he alone had penetrated the boundary defined by many as time and space. Again, the plight of all in the valley arrived at the very spot he now stood and so did the sad-sounding refrain called *Why?*

Now he felt smooth-talking his mind may be beneficial in helping him get started here. He told himself to relax and at first there was some success.

His knees he bent slightly, as if to sit on a bar stool. It soon became clear to him an easy go of it would not be his, and he backed off the shot. Again he went back into it. Nicolas set up his biased stance over the ball. He had assumed his normal two-plank strategy. Butterflies had not migrated but went south. In his stomach they had increased their flight traffic. Nicolas told himself he was about ready in an effort to instill trust.

Once again he settled into his stance. He worked at getting his feet in the preferred position. They were at equal points, though the heavier burden was on his back or right foot. He turned his left foot in some to get it more square. It felt like a weighted stone. Just do your part, his left foot seemed to tell him. We'll keep the swing tight.

Nicolas Kumar hoped for more trouble to consider. He had the feeling to stand up straighter. He went from focusing on his grip to where there was a warring battle of nerves being played out. This had him shaking like the proverbial leaf.

Once, twice, again, he moved the 3-wood back and forth while staring down at his rotund little nemesis. He hoped to get back his groove. Nicolas looked to the one hovering as an alien craft just behind the little white ball.

In a whisper that came in a quivering tone he said, 'Still I do not relish this.'

He looked again at the Valley of Flowers that was sparkling bright. All appeared fresh and alive. Trust showed and writ large on his face. Nicolas gripped the club tighter then let go some. He adjusted his posture from loose pillar to post.

The youth continued performing this bit of bad theatre for the paying-for-it flower crowd. He wondered again how he could ever reconcile hitting into this many-flowered valley.

Within himself, he settled in more. He went further into the idea of hitting this little white ball. He opened then closed his hands over the 3-wood yet again. Nicolas discovered it was not easy to grip the club with his nervous digit nerves. It might have appeared that he was holding a red-hot pipe.

He endured twelve seconds of perspiration. Inside his head he forced an *OK!* message.

Nicolas signaled his reflexes to get in and do the dirty work. He wished not to think but to allow muscle memory to take over. Then, as if ringing the doorbell twice, Nicolas held the club firmer though not too. His mind left off the effort at getting his body to stand more correctly. He told himself that he could take the swing at any time.

Again he backed off the shot. He stepped back to look at an area over the valley. He looked to the scaling, seven snow-clad mountain idols and sought resolve there. He may have had harsh feelings for the one holding up his play till now, but he readily forgave himself for this.

Nature responds to intention, he told himself, in an attempt to encourage. Just not today, his other self chided. He noted in the next instant one more thing. Nicolas believed it was not always an easy ask to give the grand okay a nudge and to just say *Yes!* to it.

With a reluctant heart, he went back in but stalled more. He hoped to get a sense the flowers were going to be okay with this. He prayed for some sign from the Upstairs. Receiving no answer he aimed to just trust.

12 | *In The Pin-Drop Silence*

Nicolas stood with his plan to send a no-hoper into the lake. His mind however created more excuses for not being able. As to how to go about hitting, Nicolas had no real idea. To him, it seemed the body of someone else stood over it. He felt ill thinking that he would be striking out into this world soon. Nicolas tried coming up with last-minute answers to a few unending questions. He argued in his head for added time. He remained at the spot as an observer, taking serious note but outwardly doing nothing. He thought this act of hitting might lay heavily on his conscience forever.

He felt Arjuna might accept this chance to ask if everything was okay with him, or would he be needing to take mental tests.

Nicolas Kumar looked at what lies ahead for him. His sad sight went to all flower locations. Images collected in his mind and he saw only horror. He felt his talent might seep out of his toes over this. Nicolas feared his game could be thrown off kilter, if indeed he went ahead with this plan to attack

He peered down at the ball. It perched comfortably atop the tee as a griffon in any tree. He looked then at the clubhead hovering behind. At first the club and ball appeared hopeful. They seemed to stare back. He wondered if these two were poking fun at him or if this situation was even real. He saw the ball and club give each a curious look. He heard in his head the ball say to the 3-wood, Who is this one with the special needs and what is he waiting for?

Another comment came as to kick him in the rear. He next imagined the flight of this one he would sometime hit.

He held the club that seemed to want nothing more than to get going. He drew his well known inner-perception lines. He repeated this again and again till the actual hitting of the ball was getting lost in all the line-sailing. Nicolas put away his sketchbook mind. He focused next on his fourth, fifth, sixth, seventh address over the ball that proved also to be just teasing. Come on, baby doll, he thought, forcing in some lightness.

He joked but took note of his inordinate delay in getting started up here. He made out he was like any Indian cinema star. He pretended to be waiting for the right script to come along before accepting the usual song-and-dance picture project. He told himself also, Either resign, retire altogether, or get on with it, sweetness.

Normally he had his school chums along for the ride as his strongest supporters. However, Nicolas was no longer in any mood for the glad-happy chatter as from the attaboys.

He chanced becoming even more miffed with himself if he did not take the shot soon. He told himself to be more alone inside. Nicolas spoke to The Protector of the Masses Lake. He wanted some assurances. He shifted his weight to be more on his right foot. The difference could be measured in tiny minute grams.

Nicolas felt things were about to get going. Opposition to this, however, mounted. More challenge came when he let go his grip some to shake off a stiff hand. The hold up in his play till now seemed all set to continue. He gazed down at the little white ball. He appeared hell bent on discovering its beginning and end.

Nicolas turned to peer out at the days-are-numbered flower crowd. He saw the soaring Indian Himalayan mountains in the background and felt their uplifting support. He looked to the spoken-to cushion of wet that was the small lake.

Yeah, I know! Nicolas yelled in his head. Hitting into the lake is not my usual intention, I got that!

Peripherally, he saw the old man shift some. He imagined Arjuna kicking a pebble or two out of sheer impatience. He heard him clear his throat to perhaps speak more. He feared Arjuna may take advantage of his stalled situation. Nicolas thought the old man might take this chance to offer more of his wisdom or his perceived bit of vague talk.

It occurred to Nicolas to hurry. He explored this idea more and his fears rose. Thought-patterns as these formed and gathered. They leapt onto this one reality.

'Now if you were to swing some time today,' said Arjuna, 'and the ball strikes that small tree there and then bounces back, the ball coming to rest a step or two behind you, is this not a progress? The shot is not forgiven, yes? No, I do not think it is, and it should not be. And I hope they never change the rule. It is a progress. It's a progress in disguise. I did not see it myself for quite a while, but I wholeheartedly believe it is. Maybe along your way you will encounter a retracing step or two. Is this not a progress? Do your duty then to the best of your abilities, for others and for yourself. Do so without selfish motive. Remember, before starting work, or at completion of some task, or now while standing so inactive, do not think of God as one and you another, as God is in All performing joyfully. Begin by understanding this. You can learn to respect this truth by repeated prayer. Look upon all creatures too as if they are you, in thought, word, and deed. In recognition of this one truth, of you as an equal, forgive yourself for any and all transgressions or blue mountains of error. The light that shines so bright that you before could hardly see, shines well within you now and will do so always. Your tears too, at any sorry sad time, which may flow as any mountain stream, are in reality unnecessary, and the sadness that you feel then only lacks true understanding. Again, forgive me. Please, continue with what you were doing.

Nicolas took in the old man’s words as cruel punishment. He told himself, I probably had that coming. It occurred to him next to make use of this interruption. He felt he could excuse himself and back off the shot.

He reversed that decision though. The youth said quietly, 'I can’t do that.' Another thought came to him. Here too he readily scotched it. Nicolas told himself also, I can't do that either.

Now he felt as fragile as any bud. Nicolas looked at the Valley of Flowers that was giving him such a torrid time. He rehearsed in his mind the scene that was already an epic by taking him forever. He tried to procure the green light.

Nicolas Kumar blocked out all audience stares. He shouted in his head, *You're stalling!*

Now he felt as nervous as any first-timer at a major. He had the idea to let all caution lie with the unpredictable wind. He heard himself say a strong *Yes!* to it. This seemed to be the thing he had been awaiting. It provided him true spark.

Put up a decent performance, Nicolas advised himself. He then added a soft-spoken, though choice set of words. After the swearing-in ceremony he felt about ready.

13 | *The Unfit Paceman*

Down from the high hills the wind occasionally blew in. It arrived out of nowhere and went away. The wind blowing in then seemed to support the theory that now was the time for this much-awaited event.

Nicolas sped through even more preoccupations in his mind. He wished to receive an *OK!* message from the Approver. It felt good knowing someone was up there thinking of him.

He peered down at the one teed up. Fear set in. Hands, he sensed, had been laid on his. Nicolas underwent last-minute checks. This included repeated glances down the flowerful fairway. Nicolas was next caught dead aplomb over the ball. He looked poor as a *fakir* while possessing not one mind possession.

He felt not yet ready to swing into action. He was surprised then to see the club was mobile. The club he had held for so long was indeed moving, and in earnest this time. It drew a faint line over the grass where dew had been.

The 3-wood went with extended care rearward. It rose. The club then looked to be scrambling up a fire ladder to save a helpless victim. It reached a peak. It was roughly at parallel. In perfect peace, the 3-wood appeared to relax by reclining. He added more stretch and the club dipped below its zenith.

As if that were the last straw, the club sharply rose from its lie-there position. The club went around then down with a to-heck-with-all fast motion. The unbearable coil reacted to the terrible tension his body had made. It sent the 3-wood crashing. The iron club, curiously referred to as a type of wood, was fast-called back to Earth. It had returned to its starting point as a metal-worker's hammer. All could hear the ball and 3-wood connect, *Ting!* The two sounded as if they had been involved in an unfortunate roadside melee.

His many-armed swing, eight-spoked, swung the 3-wood down and through. His hands swept beyond the area where the ball had been and turned over. His little grippers arrived behind his left ear. They seemed to have found a secret safe spot to hide.

The ball had shot out as a medium-pacer in this place of vanishing heights. Nicolas Kumar had put in the brakes at the bottom before hitting. Sorely missing in the attack was his usual tremendous firepower.

Yes! he said to himself, despite having serious misgivings, and the good feeling that always came to him after hitting was followed fast by an ignoble vision.

Nicolas Kumar sought the skies silently. The unfit paceman that flew lined the skies white. The ball climbed the sky as any common airliner. His drive was his heart's opposite. It was slowly inching up as his feelings for it were heading fast back down.

The ball went as a leisurenaut. It went as any life condition. It was at first expansive and ascendant. It would soon reach some peak. Then it would descend.

With cheerless intent, Nicolas watched it go. He wanted it to drop in the drink, *Kerplop!* He feared it might overshoot its target and he experienced more dampened spirits.

'Go less!' he shouted, as he remained in the follow through position.

He sent his gaze low. Nicolas believed this was the correct position for him, a future flower harvester. The wildflowers with the sweetest scents looked like upturned designer cups. They seemed made only for catching broken hearts.

Nicolas told himself added punishment would surely be his if he did not look up and follow the shot soon. He settled in again at watching. He saw in the delightful blue skies the ball vie for more space. It showed a lack of conviction for one fresh out of the box. It went into its death dive. The ball proceeded to dump down hard in the snow-melt lake, a slow-sail down into unceasing darkness. And there he saw its violent finish. Now the youth was no longer a go-getting linkster but an insurance person.

Nicolas wondered if this act might herald in an accurate prediction for his whole round up here. He thought nothing now as blankness froze him. Nicolas gazed at the spot his ball's life ended predictably wet. He looked as any shocked relative of the deceased. Eight seconds had past since his ball left the tee. It went into the Protector of the Masses Lake just as he had planned it.

Nicolas brought the club down low. He rocked the 3-wood back and forth over the given green ground. He swept the club lightly to and fro as if rocking to sleep old granny. He shook his head in a dejected way. In absence of applause, his usual appreciations, he did not tip his cap. Instead, he continued sweeping the club over the sad sorrowful ground. It seemed to him the time to till the land had just now come.

Nicolas felt weighted. For a second or so, he experienced more than an ounce of regret. He defied the six years of age that he felt he was then by bending low like the aged. He reached down and unceremoniously removed the tee from the ground. He lifted it amidst all the perceived laughter, or general *hardy-har-hars* coming up at him just then from the dull-green grass.

Again he felt separate and small. He thought of this good teacher's perceived indignation. Nicolas went to return the 3-wood to his rucksack. He walked with an award-winning performance in aloofness. Nicolas Kumar went in a silence that was vacuum-like. He said inside his head, Do it gently. This was his sole stage direction.

He took up his jacket and tied it around his waist. Nicolas raised his pack onto his right shoulder. He moved to strap in the other. His rucksack, which may have grown moss on it from the long delays, was adjusted to fit. He hopped up to even out the weight more. He stood then in jelly suspension.

Nicolas went over in his mind the tee shot that went as he had wanted. He sneaked a peek at his teacher who appeared not bothered. He considered the nonplussed look on the old man's tanned face that spoke volumes. He looked to have solved the sun.

Arjuna already had on his jacket. He picked up and then put on his small pack. He lifted his opened umbrella to work as his sunshade.

Nicolas undid the straps of his pack and he set all down. He took out his own umbrella, grey and shrunken. He opened then hoisted above him the thing that looked miserable. All sunlight from the sky suddenly left his frame briefly.

The old man adjusted his pack and he was off. He walked down the front of the tee box platform. He went without uttering a word. Arjuna went as any unpuzzled seeker. Nicolas perceived this as a slight. He felt this snub was for hitting it into the Protector of the Masses Lake. He wanted to think of something different. He told himself to remain positive. In this way he hoped to achieve some relief.

14 | *Statues of Martyrs*

Nicolas could not help but walk slope-shouldered down. His irons banged together as he stepped off the tee-block platform. Sounds of his clanging clubs came to him then as sharp criticisms. A series of *I told you so's* reverberated in his ears. The reproach entered his body unobstructed.

Pesky, chatty, his irons seemed determined to speak all at once at him. They sounded quite concerned over the plight of these flowers or statues of martyrs. His club complaints were made greater as he descended further off the elevated tee box. With each step down, his irons clamoured for him to heed their good counsel and quit this place.

Just then a shadow of his self appeared. The image was that of a black knight, dressed in all black. It extended left and behind him. The shadow trailed him outside the protective shade of his grey umbrella.

Nicolas stepped down onto the many-flowered fairway. He went into one colourful crowd, or hostile social situation that was cushion-like. He headed to the fast-flowing stream he had once found reassuring. He reached the running water as a creature might, desperate for its unique brand of salvation.

His club protests were drowned out. Sounds of the rushing stream had quieted his squad of nuisance clubs. The eternal hum of the stream dimmed too the noises going off inside his head.

The youth undid his pack then set all down. He bent low to take a sip. Afterwards he saddled up and carried on. Chants of *Om Sri Ram* played in his mind. Nicolas recited this gift, not to achieve bliss but for total distraction. He approached one batch of flowers that looked to have on guarded smiles. This was in stark contrast to the bright view he had of them on first arriving. Nicolas walked with his pack on his back as a day-labourer in pressing need. He went along the fast-flowing stream. He could see the way to cross was over an old stone bridge. The bridge appeared ancient. It looked to date back to the time of the *Mahabharata*.

Nicolas continued under his dull umbrella. He went as any sad figure might, grey in the middle of a world filled with colour. He attempted next to stride with purposeful intent. He looked to the old man. He felt a riot-like situation was at the spot Arjuna now stood. The area seemed chock-full of colour. Nicolas continued with his heavy foot action. He stomped on a multitude of flowers as he went. He crushed colour and stem, leaf and bud, with each press down of his heavy hiking boots. It may have appeared to any looking on that he was carrying out aerial target killings.

The gushing waterfall, known to the locals, the migratory shepherds, or the nomadic herders as The Fountain, became louder then with every crushing step forward.

Nicolas crossed over the old stone bridge. Moments later he reached the front of the lake or nearest point of entry of his drive. He set down his pack. He pulled from it one new ball. He searched for a suitable place to drop it. However, little clear area was found.

He extended an arm over one area that looked good enough. He let go. The ball landed fine. It rolled over to one flower group. He watched the ball cuddle up to or boyfriend one flower. The ball had stopped inches from an area he much more preferred. This was nothing new. It was often the case as with any course-goer who had quite other plans for it.

After the drop, fresh tribes of flowers appeared interested in getting close. Each stood between being a thing alive and one dead. Several pink geraniums seemed to line up to take their chances. Stunning mauve polemoniums stood prettily in his way. Others appeared waiting.

As to the mass murder about to be administered, in oblong patches, he did not care for it much. To him, the flowers were gathering, giving, benefiting and accepting, in perfect peace with all in the Valley of Flowers. He felt they were multiple bests in a grand show of winners. They looked as if it were their birthright destiny to stand there in his way.

Nicolas understood that most of the massacring was about to come. He cursed the day that he agreed to come up here for this. Again he told himself he had no real choice. He pulled from his pack his pitching wedge. He chose this club to cut through all flower clutter.

Nicolas bent back as practise the stems of one flower group. They leaned onto one another. The corralled became as one tamed. They stood captured and caged. To control these natives into revealing, he bent back their stems more. He hoped to get a better look-see too at the flowers he would sometime hit.

After more proddings, he roamed the club with some force. Soon Nicolas was sifting through a delightful series of blue forget-me-nots that were strange and mystifying. He looked back at the old man who was still searching. Nicolas saw him peer down into one brilliant patch. He scolded himself for not helping in the search.

'What were you thinking?' he said.

Then Nicolas saw that the old man had unexpectedly found it. He watched him reach down to pick up the ball. Arjuna turned in his direction. He raised the ball in apparent high triumph. He seemed the happiest of all men. The old man held it up as if match-lit. From this distance he looked like a lighthouse to eternal wisdom.

Nicolas saw him pocket it to quit. He thought this was his way of accepting his lost chance at securing par or better.

'Perhaps he is thinking that toiling on this 1st hole would be hard to take,' Nicolas said to no flower in particular. It's like bowling into the nets, his other self said inside. 'Maybe the next will be better for him,' said the first.

Arjuna, however, had different thoughts. While he enjoyed the idea of pitting himself against the vagaries of nature, other things were on his mind. He believed it best to focus on this fourth stage in life of the *sannyasi*, or wandering ascetic. He accepted his circumstances as they were. With a sense of physical ease, Arjuna sent out his consciousness to be with All in the vast Valley of Flowers.

'See the Goddess,' he said, and he had the glorious feeling of self-surrender.

Arjuna saw himself then in this other way of being, where the sun is always at the centre. The old man concentrated next on the many-coloured flowers that deserved laurels. He sensed their eternal presence. Arjuna mixed sight, sound, scent and thought that intermingled inside. He enjoyed the magic of blended senses that included touch. He sensed the grand eternal wonder by simply having enthusiasm for it.

The old man gazed at the waterfall while seeing well into another time. Eyes locked, he witnessed the existence of Is and Is Not. It added greatly to the serenity that surrounded, material and non. Forgiveness is a quality of the advancing, he thought. Then he said, *'Dhri,'* meaning uphold it together. The old man recited next under his breath a passage from one particular holy text. In return for being so mindful, the Goddess offered him yet another spectacular view.

The cascading rainbow showed its high-arching colours willingly. In attendance up there too were senior members from Arjuna's distant playing past. The old man looked to the flowers nearest him. In each he saw their everlasting presence that could never be affected. He saw in them also a sea of new horizons.

Arjuna felt free from conflict, fear, agitation, guilt, and hurt. The absorbing sight of these energetic colours gushing over the Valley of Flowers had him standing there as any true believer.

He inched towards more stillness. Through the magic of blended sight, sound, scent, touch, as well as thought, he felt the divine force's glorious presence. This re-ignited in him the sense that all is timeless eternity. He reached down to touch one idyllic leaf. He believed the flower's cup was the Abode of the Most High. He bent to hold between finger and thumb one elegant, fragile petal. Arjuna felt free from space and time. Again he sensed the divine energy.

His eyes traveled over the four cities that exist on four sides which are the cardinal directions. He saw into the astral that is so rich. A moment later he let go some of the north part that concerns health and wealth. Arjuna renounced again all attachment to worldly life. The old man vowed to act daily in this one flower's service. He came back then as on a boat to arrive at some port of call to teach the Vedic ways more.

The old man stood then as an enjoyer. He felt blessed for this illuminative experience. He was glad for this gift of being meditatively so able. For being so mindful, Arjuna was offered one more remarkable vision. The soft-spoken rainbow could again be seen. The rainbow arched as any flying-high arrow over all in this hallowed battleground.

Arjuna thought, Now is the time for doing.

He looked to the youth who seemed spoiling for a fight. He smiled at this. Arjuna moved to join this fine young fellow. He went as one who had good news to tell. Arjuna had the desire to relate the rhythm and hum of this grand eternal as best he knew it. He wanted to recount what he had only just experienced though the wish did not possess him.

To that aim, Arjuna walked towards crossing the old stone bridge or mysterious place of both arrival and departure. He went as one who can easily hold in what he had to say.

Nicolas turned to face the old man. He saw Arjuna crush scores of flowers as he went. He watched him walk through the flowered valley where even carrying plastic is a no-no. He noticed too on the old man's face that he was in no rush to instruct. Arjuna looked not in a hurry to say a thing more, and the youth relaxed some. Nicolas watched him cross the old stone bridge and then come his way.

'Surely one who is born today is sure to die,' said Arjuna, stepping over to the youth while smiling. 'And true too, all alive will live always and never have you not been.'

He appeared quite refreshed. He said, 'In time every record will dissolve away. Not one will remain. I guarantee you not one record will linger on. It is no different with a stone. When touched by the sun's spotless flame, as with running water long enough, it is sure to look like a chapati bread at the end.'

Arjuna gazed down at one flower nearest him. He looked back at Nicolas. He said, 'Now in playing this high course, I ask that you follow the flight of the sun. Each day begins on its one-wheeled chariot. The sun sets off in the east, shines in all these places north and south then comes to rest in the west, in Gujarat. The sun's spotless shine carries on its daily way to the Arabian countries. Or you can have it that, in a moment's time the sun's dawning praise signals that you are in India's east, in the age-old city of Benares perhaps, or even better Kolkata. Halfway through this cycle you are in the south, which could be in the state of Kerala. When the sun goes to rest, you are in the west. As with the course of the sun, the ball sets off and rises. It transits to arrive at some peak. Then it goes down to rest awhile.'

Arjuna held up. Something different was on his mind. The thought seemed to have familiarity. He then added, 'Willing is not enough, you must act. Know too you are asked to be courageous.'

The youth had a startling revelation. The bombshell alone appeared to speak volumes to him. The eye-opener he knew had been hinted at before. And what was giving him such a fright was that he would be going on alone up here, into the ceaseless wild.

15 | *A Ceremonial Starter*

Nicolas was surprised he would be taking this news so hard. He closed his eyes and held back his sadness. He switched from using eco-lights to looking now at the old stone bridge. In the remaining moments with this good teacher, Nicolas judged the bridge to be strong and solid. It looked to have lasted for over millennia. A normal monsoon from his eyes could at anytime be expected. The old man appeared ready to leave then when he spoke more.

'Now the number of hits you take, count them as rows of pearls, linked each-to-each, as with every breath you take in and also give back.'

The youth first thought to ask this sage what was really on his mind. Instead he throated softly, 'But will you not see me through this colourful valley?' He wished to erase then what he had only just said.

Arjuna remained silent. He thought how best to answer the youth's question. It occurred to Arjuna to say that he was at the stage when quiet contemplation, complaints, along with ever-present pain were likely to take over. He kept all that to himself, however. Instead the old man replied by sending out first a heavy sigh that sounded like extreme exhaustion.

Arjuna breathed in fully. He said, 'I am at the heartfelt most excellent stage in life. I am seventy-two, and have said my last farewell to the game. This course is yours.'

This news was something Nicolas felt might never sink in. As for being left lone up here, the idea took him to despair. He held back feelings of heartbreak. Nicolas believed he had been tasked with some strange new appointment. He concerned himself next with the way ahead. It appeared to have claimed sacred ground.

He peered at the snow-clad mountains through moist eyes. The Indian Himalayas looked like glittering colossals, fresh from a violent storm.

Again he thought to leave this paradise. Nicolas wanted to do an about-face, head back down the mountain, take the overnight bus, to enjoy once more his wild turn at play with his school chums back in the big city. He wished to be just as any fortunate city dweller: arrive at the valley then stay briefly, promise to return some day, but only after a number of years had safely gone by.

Till such times, he thought.

Nicolas next focused on this guide about to leave him. This raised his fearing speculations. He wished to know if his father had paid this guru. Nicolas Kumar wanted to know if he could treat him as one who is hired and so make him do as he wished. He felt it was this good teacher's solemn duty to stay here and guide him. I mean, why else did he come up here anyway?

He felt not present at the spot he now stood. Time ticked so slowly. This lasted until Arjuna spoke up and so decide himself that time should altogether stop.

'Think of me as an honorary starter,' the old man said. As to the time-honored tradition, the ceremonial starter is a sweet touch. It is a time to witness golf royalty.

He handed the ball back to Nicolas. He said, 'And of course there is always a teacher to help guide you.' He next gave a sweep of his arm over all in the valley. This was in playful imitation of young Nicolas from earlier.

He turned to leave. Arjuna headed towards the stone bridge. He looked back a time or two while walking. The youth's gloomy eyes posed risk of severe flooding. He experienced an upwelling. He feared falling into uncontrollable crying. Nicolas thought this was done only by the saddest saps.

He held out hope things might change for the noticeable better. It occurred to him this teacher could see him crying. Nicolas felt it would be a clear directive for Arjuna to stay longer. And so he let go, allowing the dams to break.

Nicolas open-carried his heart as if on his sleeve, blood-red and beating. To this water-shedding, a precious commodity up in these mountains, strange considering so much rain, he could not then see out. His expression of sorrow reached a peak. He tried clearing up his sight. He saw that Arjuna had not returned but was instead some distance off. Still blurry, he watched Arjuna step up onto the old stone bridge. He saw the old man stop on the bridge's crest. He watched Arjuna raise his hand then in a casual goodbye.

Next thing Nicolas knew was that this teacher, this humble guide and good friend to him here, would not be coming back.

He felt the sudden pang of some departure. Nicolas was then a bit shame-faced for outwardly crying. With no good counsel to see him along his way, the image of his father made a brief though surprise visit.

He saw his father atop the old stone bridge. His father had on the same stern look when Nicolas left home to come up here. This visit too would end in heart-wrenching pain. He saw his father raise up his arm further in a gesture of fond farewell. Nicolas raced through a series of past memories. He noticed the old man's bracelet, a white ouroboros, or world-girdling serpent, worn round his wrist as a gentle reminder to eternal return, slide down not his father's arm but Arjuna's.

'But how shall I find this honorable teacher?' Nicolas cried out, in an effort to get back, as tears rolled down his cheeks.

'Easy!' called Arjuna, and his mischievous grin was again on his tanned face. He reminisced atop the old stone bridge for a moment or two. All grown up, the old man sported his boyish smile. He then yelled out to the youth, 'This chant I leave you with!'

Naughty and witty, Arjuna hollowed his raised hand. He put his hand to his mouth. The old man did this to guide the vibration of his resonating deep voice. Almost magically, the colours of the Kundalini showed brilliantly behind him. Colours as these appeared all round. By miraculous grace, the grand mark of time too shined. The Grand Chronocator sun spread a ring of gold light over all in the spectacular Valley of Flowers.

Arjuna breathed in deep. He seemed ready to bellow a glad tiding with his trumpeting loud voice. Nicolas understood that the old man's future comment would be meant for him to draw from here, as well as for years after. He knew, too, that it would likely end this major scene between them.

'Look for one who is wide-eyed and wanders freely!' the old man shouted. And again he sported a boyish smile that many have said could push up mountains.

Arjuna bent down to touch the old stone bridge in a gesture of *darshan*. He crossed over the bridge. He reached the far side of the stream, or nascent new ocean that now separated them. Again Arjuna opened and then hoisted above him his multi-coloured umbrella. He began heading back to a life of joyous austerity, ascent through descent, by way of a path made up of colourful wildflowers.

Nicolas watched him go. He saw this peerless mentor climb the short rise to arrive back up onto the 1st tee of this high course known as

Truind. He watched him go back behind a small hillock there. Then he was out of sight. Nicolas stared at the spot lit up by a prettifier sun. The departure of this good teacher left him feeling so alone.

16 | *A Stroke Penalty*

He wore a deserted look. Nicolas prepared in his heart for more flower destruction. He stood unmoving, looking as if he were a physicist doing time-solving. He attempted next to make light. The one who is an *anātha*, or orphan without a guiding teacher, said again he regretted getting out of bed for this. He turned to look at what lay ahead for him. In his grief, he saw that Nature seemed exceedingly restless.

Nicolas surveyed a white flag on a white flagstick. The flag on the green stood beyond the flowers and snow-melt lake. It fluttered in the breeze faithless. The white flag pointed at the ground. This told him he should just lie down and wait for vultures.

He considered the flag's suggestion for him. Nicolas stood for a time staring. He appeared afflicted by the three-fold miseries: arising from the body itself, by other beings also, and by natural occurrence. He dwelt more on the nature of defeat. Then his nerves moved on some to steel city.

'Time to move into action,' he said.

He thought of the ball he had dropped no further than one club length from the point of entry. Nicolas went to stand over the ball. He set up then to hit it with the club he already had. He held out in front of him the same pitching wedge. He gripped the club like the law was in his hands.

Next thing he knew a dozen or so flowers shot up from the drop zone. They had flown up from his *Swoosh!* swing.

The thing was over in a flash. It made him look like an avid embroidery trader. The ball had left the spot medium-like. It had crossed the Protector of the Masses Lake though off to one side. It instantly headed into a flowerful bouquet as a failed missile. He felt vandalistic, a 21st-century heretic.

He looked to where a bundle of flowers lay complementary to this very idea. He went to stamp down on these little beauties while not really wishing to. Nicolas bent to pick up his pack. He struggled to put it on properly. A yellow-throated marten scurried by. Nicolas Kumar tried following the path of this unlikely running visitor. He thought to catch a ride on its tiny body and escape from this place. But as suddenly as this one animal appeared it went away. Then the flight of another arrived. The grim shadow of this flier raced over the reluctant flower ground.

In place of looking up, Nicolas followed its unsettling running shadow. The grey silhouettes produced grotesque shapes over the many-coloured valley. The gross images went in quick, undulating rolls. He looked up to spot it. This flier, or one on duty up in the guard tower, had left the area before he could catch any glimpse of it, other than what rolled ugly over the many-flowered valley. In his head he called it The Bachelor.

Nicolas Kumar went to the spot near the lake where his ball had gone. He found it without too much difficulty. The ball was resting up against a gathering of pink flowers. He laid down his pack. He then pulled from it one club and set up. A second or so later he took the club back. Flowers ripped up. They flew off in quick dispersion. His swinging looked done by a farmer's pitchfork bailing hay. It seemed to him that he had only come here to tear this world apart.

Nicolas picked up his pack and headed to the place his ball had flown. He found it in a difficult spot. It occurred to him next to just kick the thing. He felt he could improve his lie this way. Nicolas Kumar hesitated and in the end he did not.

Another swing came and went. This too was done by his earth-remover pitching wedge. The ball rode the air briefly. Mountain peaks showed up as magnificent backdrops. They were the models of beauty to anyone.

Nicolas went the short way to where his ball lay. Again he had the notion to do some form of ball-tampering. He felt it would be easy enough to give the thing a spot-kick or roll it over with the bottom of his hiking boot. Nicolas thought he could roll it up onto a tuft of something not so petaled. But then he decided against it. Nicolas said in a voice unlike his own, '*Devabhumi*. Remember, you are on God's land.'

Soon after he took one horizontal swing. Nicolas took back the club as a flattened practise stroke. He rode the flat line once, twice, again. He swung once more at a similar angle as Ben Hogan's well known one-plane swing. He took aim with his eyes first. Nicolas gripped the club again and again. He tried finding even a crumb of cold comfort.

Nicolas listened then was treated to the thrashing sound his swing had made at hard impact. He gathered his things and went to where his ball had landed near more delicate flower petals. Again he set up. He swung. The shot came out fat. It went a short way with the seemingly worthless material known as common dirt.

The ball had gone in one colourful patch. It had fallen into flowers shaped as upturned stars. He looked down. Nicolas saw that the flower dead were many. His swinging in the area had claimed lives. Countless were seriously wounded. The fresh scars on the ground looked like after-effects of a crude bomb. The disappearance of these flowers seemed sorely missed by the remaining others. Nicolas told himself that the stroke penalty for hitting in the lake was something he needed to remember.

He went to the place his shot had gone. He looked for his ball with his pack still on his back. Nicolas felt the flowers might remarkably spill the beans as to where his friend was by simply telling him. In his ears the whispering grapevine had it that his ball had nestled in nicely.

Nicolas got word it had found good accommodation in among their bunch. The flowers seemed to say, or perhaps it was just his intuition, that his ball was off right. He turned his offending wedge in that direction. He stood tall in the fight. His cap was in his free hand when abruptly he pointed with it with keen relish.

'There!' he said.

He set down his pack of club boys to one side. Nicolas put back the club and pulled out a different wedge. In this way he showed his firm intention of taking up arms in the valley. He returned his cap on his head. He took two swings above his found ball. Nicolas stood blank, became lost as any wild hare. Now he felt all were hunting him and that this was his own elimination round.

For his next turn at destruction, he had chosen a lob wedge. He took a swing above the spot his ball lay comfortably in the mix. Nicolas set up in earnest and in a flash the ball was away. It rose with a splashed bundle of flower growth. All took off heavy with a thick slab of moist earth.

Nicolas watched all fly. The mud-as-divot flew off with the flowers. The divot soon gave up its struggle for life through flight then flopped down. He focused next on the place his ball went. Into more clusters he had sent this sad story. He looked at the spot of his ball's previous predicament. He felt he should replace the divot or at least clean up some the manhole he had only just created. It occurred to him next that the area could end up ranking highest in destruction of any Indian state. He swung angry at the air. He believed he was doing less damage this way.

His club hovered next over a few flower bulbs. He focused his sight on the ball. Nicolas next looked to be in the midst of a murderous frenzy when he took the swing. After which, he picked up his pack. It was loaded onto his right shoulder as if hurtling bodies onto a dead-cart. He headed to another group of mingling flowers where his ball lay in the mix. He found his ball, thanked God, then he laid down his heavy pack. He went to take the shot. He moved to set up. Soon another explosive batch of flowers was all he knew.

Nicolas watched all go. Again, he looked down at the spot his ball had been and saw only horror. The area appeared to have witnessed war firsthand. Many flowers lay dead. Pleas from the remaining others could at anytime be expected. He picked up his things and the feeling of joy was not his.

Once more Nicolas went to his ball. On finding it, he began to set up. Soon another bundle flew with an oblong moist slab of soil. Shot after shot then kept the scoreboard in the sky ticking over.

Of this killing he asked himself, Who are you to do this?

Again he picked up his kit and bore the pain of dozens. He went while the remaining others seemed to scream over the bodies of their near and dear ones.

Nicolas arrived and not long after another swing ploughed through as practise. He swung at flower shafts in repeated splash manner. He perceived the valley in vast turmoil. He drew back his destructive club to strike the ball. His wrists he set early. The club rose to the point that was roughly at parallel. He felt its powerful coil.

His many-armed motion, eight-spoked, came striking in a flash. A *Whoosh!* could then be heard cutting through. The ball, with another batch of flowers, was alight. All flew off low in abbreviated flight that descended off right. The ball flew into a ghostly haunt of tall white flowers, Brahma Kamals, that he would rather not think about.

Nicolas struggled more with life issues. He went to what would otherwise have been an easy mid-pitch to the green. This too would sail only a second or so. The ball would go sleepless into yet another flowerbed. Nicolas discovered the spot his ball lay. The youth went about making one more demarcation trench in the given flower ground. The flowers appeared to know that they were in the unenviable position of being at the mercy of this one little human.

He swung. All lost their heads while the youth did what he could to keep his own melon thinking rationally. Again he hoped to leave this trail of death and destruction. Nicolas followed the short flight of the ball. He made a mental note as to where it had landed. He gathered up his things as if to haul them off to prison. Nicolas went to where he thought his ball was and found it easily.

'Just one more hack at it and I should be on,' he said.

Several determined swings later, a rash of flop shots, and the valley was thoroughly reaped away. Now he was in no mood for sparing anyone.

Two more shots came down on the earth heavy. He neared the green and set up. He took yet another shovelful of mud, killing a handful of flowers. This try too was a flop shot.

Nicolas went with his pack the short way where his ball lay lifeless near the green. He set all down. He resisted taking a stab at it but soon it was away. He noted that the shot was one of his better ones. The ball had landed on the green and he felt happy. The green might as well have been decorated with festive lights at the time of Diwali.

He went to retrieve his things. He led his gang of ignorant thugs through traffic snarls made of colourful wildflowers. Nicolas arrived onto this dance floor green shoulders first. He stepped onto this new frontier, or elevated putting table, as a grand recipient of some award.

'Finally!' he said.

Nicolas eyed the white flag on the white flagstick. The two had a seen-it-all-before manner. The flag as Mr. Surrender looked especially sad or sorry. It seemed to say there was no reason to celebrate either light or life. The flag appeared to be telling him that there was no real reason to try.

17 | *Father Electric*

The surface of the green did not have the pleasurable pool table look he was used to. It was drawn in brown more than he would have liked. It looked thrown here and there with a type of masala chili powder. The green had a bumpy flow to it that made it look makeshift or temporary. It was thick in areas with genuine rough patches, the result of being without regular proper maintenance. He guessed the putt to be somewhere in the neighbourhood of forty feet. It was a downhiller and somewhat bending.

Nicolas gauged the putt to be a difficult one. He conceded the battle was not yet over. The flag kicked up. It fluttered in the breeze faithless. As to his chances of getting the ball up close, he felt about the same as the flag. He went to the back of the green and laid his pack on what is commonly termed the fringe.

He set all down near a few poppy swells. His pack with his clubs lay on the ground looking dazed and confused. This was in contrast to the wildflowers standing bolt upright. They stood at military attention as if their security level had just been raised a hue.

He undid his jacket from around his waist and he laid it on his pack. Nicolas pulled off the glove on his left hand. He bent down and removed the club that usually attends to any difficulty atop a green. Nicolas gripped the putter again and again. The grip seemed to have turned into a string of goat meat that just now needed tenderizing.

He went to the hole and plucked the flagstick from the cup. The hole seemed to be the usual dimensions. It looked to be 108mm in diameter by nearly 108mm deep by regulation. The repeated 108 number struck him then as quite curious.

Nicolas pulled the flag from the hole and he did not toss it. He held the flag out in front of him as if it were a baton and he was leading a parade. He laid the flagstick on the green, though well away from his line. He went to look at his putt from the far side of the hole. Nicolas thought of the magic 108 number that was the same number on the mala beads. He recalled there are 108 points that help define the human body, as with being the full range of human emotions. He remembered 108 is the number of the *Yantra*, the geometric figure that is a crucial aid to knowing Ultimate Truth.

He walked the full length of his putt then he came back. He squatted behind the ball about two meters or so. He took a long learning look at his putt. Nicolas ran an imaginary line from his ball to the cup and then back again. He focused on the grass to complete this triad known as the *Trimurti*. The cosmic functions of birth-life-death were all there with him then when abruptly he stood.

Nicolas went to the subterranean dark hole then came back. Once more he squatted low as any vegetable seller. He was directly behind the one about to be consumed. Nicolas rose. He studied the line from this roughly six-foot aerial angle.

He went back to pacing the length of his putt that appeared serpentine. He again arrived behind the ball then squatted. He inched closer. Nicolas did this to get an even finer line. He asked for divine help and stood. He moved to set up but backed off. He returned to his usual two meters behind the ball to recheck. Again, he squatted low. He rested the club on one thigh. The club with the lead tape stuck on its back, referred to by him as Father Electric, was the real deal. Of his many club weapons, this was the one he could truly rely. He was fond of this producer of winning memories. It was known for getting him good results.

Nicolas looked at the logo burnt in the club's side. It had been forged by one of golf's well-known hardware merchants.

He raised his hands to the sides of his cap as to put on blinders. His line to the hole was something of a sidewinder. He figured the right-to-left breaker would open up at the hole. He then began creating his usual line pre-enactments.

Nicolas walked the length of the putt as an inspector might looking for clues. He returned as if he'd gotten a whispered tip-off from a reliable source. He moved to take his usual stance over the ball. Suspense entered. He hoped to knock it in on one and be done with the thing.

He took a few practise strokes. Nicolas put behind the ball the club about to make its directorial début. He brought his right foot up to the spot it had been previously. As to the other, he moved it forward to be more in line with the first. He bent over more in his usual familiar putting style. He appeared all set to close some big real estate deal. Nicolas looked forward to the ball falling into the cup that might serve symbolically the cosmic function of Shiva, or Lord of Destruction, purist example yet all nature is holy.

The thought of peering into the dark cup ruled him. Nicolas held firm the club designed for such a subtle touch. He said in a tiny whisper, 'I pray only for your kindness, Lord.'

Now he felt he should get down to work. He wanted to get the proper line and speed of the green. He hoped to be done with the thing and finally. A *Quiet, please!* order seemed to have been issued to all in the valley. A hush fell onto this hard-to-believe landscape. Only the rushing stream and the occasional sounds of light air gusts could then be heard.

A strong breeze rushed in then to shove him forward. It left without much success. Nicolas adjusted his stance to settle in again. He turned the face of the club to aim a taste right for more break. He again scoped the line. Numerous looks at the hole, then over the green, then back down at the ball, would soon set all in motion. Then he just stroked it. The ball ventured off. It went as any happy-go-lucky, tra-la-la, towards the intended target where results can surely range.

Nicolas had a focused calm while watching. He observed the jolly roller travel somewhat downhill. He saw it enter a difficult spot. It had rolled into a patch of collected dirt. He demolished down any high hopes for it by thinking up the worst. The ball stopped well short of the hole. It had gotten caught up in the thick area, a pebbly beach tiny island

Nicolas took no time now in setting up over this next putt. He made the risky decision to go for it with some speed.

Give it a chance! he told himself.

Soon after, the rounded one was on its merry way. It was heading towards the cylindrical dark hole but a taste right. It turned nicely then, and against the odds. Nicolas Kumar saw the ball move onto a better line. It looked as if it could still change lanes.

Although it was by no means a shoe-in, it did look good to him. The ball went as any Good Samaritan. It broke onto an even better line. It headed directly towards the hole then. It occurred to him his putting had not lost its sheen.

Now his thoughts raced from doubt to genuine possibility. He believed the God touch might still be his.

Nicolas watched it roll along the grass not sensing his own struggle standing. Without knowing it, he began lofting his putter in celebratory anticipation. He lifted the club up bit by slow bit with ever-growing assurance.

'*Yes!'* he said aloud.

At the hole, the ball did not go in dead centre. It had turned at the end. It had spun from centrifugal force around the top curvature condition of the hole. The ball did a complete 360. It stopped and appeared to stagger on the lip of the cup. The ball looked like any sad wayfarer, standing on a street-side curb.

Nicolas hastened a low groan. He was next on the cusp of bursting into a tall flame of fire. He pleaded to the sky for guidance. Again, Nicolas felt sorry for coming up here for this. The ball looked as if it could stay atop that hard edge forever.

In place of dropping in, the ball rested atop the rim of the cup comfortably. It looked satisfied between being a thing dead and in the hole and one alive and on top. It stayed on that fine line between here and then gone. Repeated sharp looks at it did improve the situation. He felt the ball was intent on spiting him. To him, the ball had turned traitor.

He added an undesirable remark in his mind. The agony of his play to now, coupled with this close-but-no-cigar effort, came to him then as a pair of seeing-red charging bulls. He looked on the boil. A hectic lobbying for allies followed. He was dumbfounded, bitter at being left lone up here and standing there haggling with no one.

Nicolas stared at the ball. He could not comprehend how it could make such a lovely turn at the hole, then have the appalling gall not to drop in. He could not believe how it could do such a thing to him, an otherwise gentle fellow. The ball seemed hell bent on inflicting him pain. To him, it appeared Nature was designed to pin down any course-goer, as something of a rule of thumb.

Once more he decided against using anger. He knew anger would deprive the mind of correct rational thinking. He chose not to do with his club what he had done in circumstances such as this, which was plant it. Nicolas felt he had only one option. He began the mature process of letting his shadow do some of the dirty work. He moved to put his self between the sun, the ageless wonder here, and dark hole. He stood between the one in the sky burning bright and the ball or object that frequently disobeys. He felt the ball and hole might still be united in a type of matrimony, with attendees enjoying a brief show of an eclipse of the sun.

Except for where his ball lay now, the swarming sunrays were successful in covering all in the Valley of Flowers. The ball stayed atop the cup as the great Spaniard's in '84.

Just then he glimpsed a wish-fulfilling wobble.

Like preceding the birth of time, the ball appeared to quiver. A blaze of sunshine showed over the cup. Nicolas Kumar had moved from excitement but was soon back in position. He stood in the sun's light and froze. It dawned on him that he had entered a new era. He felt he still had some chance.

18 | *The Enjoyer*

Nicolas no longer felt in control of his mind. He felt he had little control over his body, too. As to what his physical self might do next, he could not be certain: toss up his cap, kick up a leg, go into a Scottish jig even, if the thing dropped in. And the ball did remain shaky. It continued balancing atop the lip of the cup. The ball kept up its devil dance known to him now as The Great Tease.

Despite his strong wish for it, the ball looked unwilling to roll over and just die. It seemed ready to continue its death dance in front of him forever. It remained atop the lip of the cup for a full four, five, six seconds, or entire length of all eternity.

But then the ball did move, and against the odds.

Then it happened. All at once, in a slow counter-rotational spiral that kept the suspense alive, the ball lost its struggle for life against death. It plunged in the cylindrical dark cup that was time-like. It fell beneath a sky lit ablaze by the sun or the all-seeming uncaring. Into this end-state the little white ball disappeared, pure and for keeps.

A quaint tumbling tune could then be heard. It sounded as if a certain someone had become somewhat bitter. The ball had been safely scuttled away and his muscles loosened. He no longer wore a long face but was actually beaming. Any could see that the ball falling in was widely appreciated by him. On his face too was a satisfied look of hard won glory.

Nicolas complimented himself on a job well done. As the big bout was now over, he felt the urge to give all a good finishing punch. He enlisted an uppercut fist-pump and his spirits soared. Nicolas went over to the hole. He gave his pant leg a hike then bent low. He reached into the dark hole, rumoured to be inhabited by snakes, ghosts, goblins, and he plucked out his roped-in ball.

He took from the cup the principle member in this drama of the absurd that had ended just fine. Nicolas extended this moment out of the sheer enjoyment of it. His happiness knew no bounds. He felt he had come through this as any talent-hunt winner.

He went to return the white flagstick to the hole. The youth headed back then to his pack sensing the tactile pleasure of repeatedly turning over the ball in his hand. Nicolas twirled between his fingers the club he held in the other. This was his favourite after-show. He then went to his rucksack as if he had all along been his own greatest cheerleader.

He returned his ball in his bag and also Arjuna's. Nicolas put away his glove and then took out his course journal. He began recounting the shock treatment he had just given this high place. He went to the page he felt his score should go. It looked entirely innocent but was about to be marred.

Nicolas recounted the number of shots he took on behalf of this curiously happy victor. The math complete, he marked down the quite high number. He picked up his jacket and tied it around his waist. He lifted his pack and returned the putter. He straightened the club's head in the bag. He set off for the 2nd without benefiting from a returning glance. Nicolas thought little of the violence he had administered over the Valley of Flowers. He thought only now of getting back his mood-making self belief or mojo.

The freshness of the air was then on his face as he dreamed of future accomplishments here. After an hour of walking, he felt he could see the 2nd in the distance. He was glad to find it without much searching here and there.

'Just a little ways more to go now,' he said aloud.

He felt he had all by himself found this next hole. He made out that he alone had discovered this next station-in-charge. He gave no recognition to the help he had received along the way. Nicolas had all along followed a narrow goat trail, set there eons ago by migrating herders. Discovering the 2nd was made possible too by it simply being there. Nature had supplied a way for him to go and would do so always.

Nicolas Kumar moved to retrieve the water bottle from his pack. He wished to give himself this fine reward. At first he struggled some with the bottle's cap. But soon it popped open and the waterworks were fully operational.

He took a drink and savoured. He got the reviving sense from this refreshment. Nicolas Kumar came back from this ecstasy additionally pumped. He held the bottle by his side and stared blankly. He looked to the Himalayas, or spread out view of heaven with renewed energy. He felt fortified and altogether good about himself. He yearned too for a return to the normal. Still, he looked forward to more play up here.

The true death toll over the valley would go uncounted. Of this he was not at all concerned. Instead, he was all over again happy with his changed form. The youth looked to where there was nothing made mechanical by man. Nicolas peered at what he believed was the 2nd tee. The hole looked quite untouched. It was without the flower concentration as on the 1st. Nicolas could not say, hand on heart, if this was indeed better. Less flowers was a good thing, he thought. But then he wondered what more might come.

He daydreamed the 1st had been easy for him. It was not at all long, he thought. He came up next with the idea of being handed a brilliant bouquet for simply participating up here. He thought to say, to any interested in hearing it, what his self was now telling him, and the message was that it would be foolish to bet against him.

He missed his gizmos. His computer and tablet he had left at home. His gaming devices were left at his family's haveli. His phone too was back in his room where he had been told to leave it. Growing up as a gadgeteer, he wished to have at least one of these with him.

As for the applause that always followed him, loud, clear in his ears and straight through early childhood, he heard even more. He felt nothing now of being immaculately whipped on the 1st. He thought only of the thing that happened at the end, when his ball dropped in. Nicolas issued a word of caution for his gloating. He brushed that aside, however, as if caution was a mere clod of dirt stuck to his pant legs.

Nicolas concentrated next on the series of standing-O's he usually received and was just now taking delivery. Sounds of virulent golf claps swelled his head. It felt like crackling sparklers had been lit and were bursting all round. He heard endless praise of himself. He enjoyed this as any fanboy.

He basked more in this glory. He felt these audience cheers were like roars of thunder. He heard loud and clear in his head the insistent calls of *"Autograph, please!"* From this crowd's incredible root-for, it was clear to him they wanted to see more.

He attempted to lift his mind above seeming street level. He focused on getting to that No. 2 spot. He walked in high triumph. Nicolas believed he cut a striking figure. He felt he looked as good as any Indian cinema star. He reached up to touch his chin. Nicolas felt for a five o'clock shadow before midday. Failing this, he lifted his cap as to acknowledge the appreciation of the imaginary flower crowd. He let loose his star-plus hair. His hair fell over his ears but hung a bit above the shoulders area. His hair went to and fro with his extended strides. He returned his cap atop his head. Nicolas Kumar flashed at all a brilliant smile. In this way he hoped to convey his immeasurable greatness.

No longer a beanpole from his earlier school days, but lean and muscular, he could not help but think he was the one doing the saving up here. The one with the grey-green eyes, and tendency to outward identify, came up next with the idea that he alone was the one to carry on to win over like the whole world. With almost no memory of his play up to now, Nicolas felt he could still achieve a good round. He had the feeling all might be okay. He said aloud to no one, 'For me to bear down now and deliver would be quite satisfying.

He next imagined there would be the equivalent of a vanity van, ready and waiting for him. But there was none. No one was waiting to whisk him off, to be interviewed perhaps by the world's adoring media. Nicolas would have to do all the footwork on his own.

Still he felt he can achieve headlines, and do so even from up here at this faraway mountain place.

Nicolas neared the 2nd tee. He stayed quiet while walking. He peered up at the Indian Himalayas or massed-up humble giants, set there forever, and which have long been a source of inspiration to so many. Although now he felt he was the one others should look up to.

He distanced himself further. Nicolas went to a spot in his I-making mind. He hibernated in this dream world. As to what he had perceived over the valley, the various applause, the appreciations, coming as from the colourful gatherings, all seemed hushed now, and waiting anxiously, in his silent support. By his recent modest play here, two putts, Nicolas felt he had rendered all quiet: breeze-blown trees, rustling brush, humbler folk, his audience.

Keep your mistakes to a minimum, Nicolas advised himself inside, as he approached the walk-up to the 2nd tee, and he felt he would be perfect from here on out.

But then he sensed in his legs the effort put in from even this mild climbing. He experienced the struggle and strain from moving in these high mountains, tall and immovable. While breathing heavily, from walking up further into thin air, his happiness with himself stayed, undaunted within him. His pride too, in his perceived achievements on the course till now, along with how good he felt he looked, left him quiet though still there. Consequently, Nicolas had no sense yet of losing himself in the presence of All. Had it not been for his strained breathing, which just now held his fascination, along with the soreness he felt in his shoulders, back, arms and legs, the daily sensations of any cart-puller, he might have gone on to spout his own versions of Ultimate Truth.

His attention turned then to the great unlimited. On the 2nd tee terrace, having finally arrived, Nicolas could see, in the far-off distance, the shimmering expanse that was the vast plains of Mother India, and he marvelled. The moment he saw this liquid gold light, it filled his heart and dissolved there, his chest and lungs deep-repeating, expressing joyfully the primal energy that is, soundlessly speaking through him, to Her, the Divine Mother, source of inner peace and strength, bestower of the highest treasures: evenness of mind, a balanced point of view, steadiness in all situations, in harmony with All in complete self-surrender.

Nicolas gazed at this sight in astonished wonder. A thought came to him. He smiled at this. He said, 'This is Brahma and this is love.'

Nicolas stood then as an enjoyer. Fueled by a humbled heart and renewed faith in this trek, his future unknown to him yet but onward, he entered into a state of all-pervading joy and wellness. And he was happy then. Grateful.

Author’s Note

“I was a surf rat from sunny Southern California who happened to play competitive golf as a teenager. Around that time, behind the ropes at Pebble Beach’s 18th green, I saw Arnold Palmer step out of a bright white scorer's booth at a pro event, his face was tanned and he was radiating charisma. It vividly reminded me of Cary Grant’s anecdote of spotting a tan Douglas Fairbanks on a transatlantic ocean liner—a moment Grant described as one of ‘casual magnificence.’

Years later, inspired, I began scribbling down this novella as my humble tribute to Palmer, and by extension golf’s legendary ‘Big Three’—Palmer, Jack Nicklaus, and Gary Player.

As I struggled to shape the story, I perhaps impulsively sent an unfinished version to Arnold Palmer himself. To my surprise, he wrote back, graciously apologizing for the delay in replying—explaining he had been 'out West,' traveling the Pacific Coast, before returning home to Pennsylvania. Touched by his generosity, I wrote this into the narrative, letting Arjuna, the novella’s wise guide, inspired in part by Palmer, urge the protagonist Nicolas to follow the daily flight path of the sun westward.

This novella, then, is not only a literary experiment but also my small offering of gratitude to those who inspire simply by being themselves.”

Chris Collins is from Santa Barbara, California

Glossary: Key Concepts & Terms

Term (Language Origin) Definition, Contextualized for the Novella

Anātha (Sanskrit) A person without protection or guidance; an orphan. Nicolas feels like an *anātha* after his guide departs.

Asan (Sanskrit) A stable and comfortable physical posture used in yoga for meditation.

Benares Silk (Geographical/ Material) Quality silk, historically woven in or around Benares (Varanasi), India. Arjuna uses this to refer to the luxurious quality of ideal fairways.

Bhagavad Gita (Sanskrit) A foundational Hindu scripture, a 700-verse text that is part of the epic *Mahabharata*. The novella *VOF* reimagines *The Gita*'s core philosophical conflict.

Brahma (Sanskrit) The creator god in the Trimurti (Hindu trinity). The *City of Brahma* is a term for a celestial, perfect realm.

Brahma Kamal (Hindi) A white, high-altitude flower (*Saussurea obvallata*), revered in Hinduism as a divine, ghostly symbol.

Chapati (Hindi) Thin, flat, unleavened bread, a staple in South Asian cuisine.

Darshan (Sanskrit) The act of seeing and being seen by a holy person, deity, or sacred sight; a moment of auspicious view.

Devabhumi (Sanskrit) A Sanskrit and Hindi term meaning "Land of the Gods," referring to the sacred Himalayan region.

Devadatta (Sanskrit) A massive conch shell and name of the conch blown by Arjuna in the *Mahabharata*.

Dharna (Hindi) A non-violent form of protest, like a sit-in or strike, often used to stage a demand.

Dhri (Sanskrit) A word meaning "to uphold, support, maintain." Arjuna uses it in the sense of holding things together.

Fakir (Arabic/Hindi) Muslim ascetic or beggar, often a wandering religious devotee. Nicolas looks poor as a *fakir* when lost in thought.

Gharana (Hindi/Urdu) A system of social organization linking musicians or dancers by lineage or apprenticeship, particularly in Hindustani classical music.

Googly (Cricket Slang) A deceptive bowling delivery designed to fool the batsman; used here to describe Arjuna's unpredictable and surprising bad shot.

Hooch Tragedy (Indian English) Severe medical incident, usually resulting in death, caused by drinking illegally or illicitly brewed alcohol (*hooch*).

Juggernaut (English from Sanskrit) A massive, relentless force or object that crushes anything in its path. Nicolas Kumar refers to the *juggernaut of live wire* in the city.

Kirana Store (Indian English) A local corner grocery or provision shop in India.

Lathi (Hindi) Heavy stick or rod, often bamboo, used as a weapon by police or guards (a baton).

Lathicharge (Indian English) Police action in which *lathis* (batons) are used to disperse a crowd.

Mahabharata (Sanskrit) One of two major Sanskrit epics of ancient India (the other is the **Ramayana**). The novella reimagines its core philosophical conflict.

Mala Beads (Sanskrit) String of beads used in Hindu, Buddhist or Jain practices, traditionally having 108 beads for counting mantras or prayers.

Masala (Hindi/Urdu) A term for a blend of spices.

Moksha (Sanskrit) Liberation or freedom from the cycle of death and rebirth (samsara), a key goal in Hinduism.

Mount Meru (Sanskrit) Highly sacred, five-peaked mountain of cosmology in Hinduism, Buddhism, Jainism, considered the centre of all physical and spiritual universes.

Ouroboros (Greek Symbol) Ancient symbol depicting a serpent or dragon eating its own tail, representing eternal cyclical renewal or eternal return.

Paceman (Cricket Slang) Fast bowler (pitcher) in cricket. Nicolas refers to his slow-moving shot as an *unfit paceman.*

Piththoo (Hindi/ Indian English) A person hired to carry heavy luggage or a passenger up a mountain trail; a porter.

Prana, Vyana, Apana (Sanskrit Three of the five vital airs or life forces (*Vayus*) in yoga: *Prana* (inward energy of the breath), *Vyana* (circulatory energy), and *Apana* (downward/eliminating energy).

Sannyasi (Sanskrit) A person who has fully renounced worldly life and entered the fourth and final stage of life (asceticism). Arjuna is in this stage.

Sclaffed (Scots/Golf Slang) To hit a golf ball with poor contact, scraping the ground with the clubhead before or as it hits the ball.

Shiva (Sanskrit) The destroyer/transformer god in the Trimurti. His destruction is necessary for creation.

Teledensity (Telecommunications) The number of telephones (or, in modern context, internet/mobile connections) per 100 inhabitants. Nicolas uses this term to note the remote nature of the valley.

Trimurti (Sanskrit) The trinity of supreme divinity in Hinduism: Lord Brahma (The Creator), Lord Vishnu (the Preserver), and Lord Shiva (The Destroyer).

Truind (Fictional Setting) Name of the high mountain golf course in the novella *VOF* where the story takes place.

Unbegun (Literary Term) Nicolas Kumar's state of refusal to start the game; used metaphorically to suggest he has not begun his real, destined task.

Vedas (Sanskrit) The most ancient Hindu scriptures, containing hymns, philosophy, and guidance on ritual.

Yantra (Sanskrit) Geometric diagram that functions as a tool for meditation and spiritual contemplation.

Literary analysis of Valley of Flowers novella here:

* Valley of Flowers: The Paradox of Beauty (500 pages)
* Valley of Flowers: A Panoramic Ironic Eden (330 pages)
* Valley of Flowers: A Duel in the Sun (240 pages)
* No Recipe for Pancakes (200 pages)

Valley of Flowers novella (30,011 words)

Reviews are helpful.

www.ingramcontent.com/pod-product-compliance
Lightning Source LLC
Chambersburg PA
CBHW070344130626
46556CB00007B/3019

* 9 7 8 0 9 8 2 3 9 4 9 6 0 *